Karin Baine lives in Northern Ireland with her husband, two sons and her out-of-control notebook collection. Her mother and her grandmother's vast collection of books inspired her love of reading and her dream of becoming a Mills & Boon author. Now she can tell people she has a *proper* job! You can follow Karin on Twitter, @karinbaine1, or visit her website for the latest news—karinbaine.com.

Also by Karin Baine

Reforming the Playboy
Their Mistletoe Baby
From Fling to Wedding Ring
Midwife Under the Mistletoe

Single Dad Docs collection

Tempted by Her Single Dad Boss
by Annie O'Neil
Resisting Her English Doc
by Annie Claydon
The Single Dad's Proposal
Nurse to Forever Mum
by Susan Carlisle

Discover more at millsandboon.co.uk.

THE SINGLE DAD'S PROPOSAL

KARIN BAINE

MILLS & BOON

First published in Great Britain 2019
by Mills & Boon, an imprint of HarperCollins*Publishers*
1 London Bridge Street, London, SE1 9GF

Large Print edition 2019

© 2019 Karin Baine

ISBN: 978-0-263-07838-1

MIX
Paper from
responsible sources
FSC™ C007454

This book is produced from independently certified
FSC™ paper to ensure responsible forest management. For
more information visit www.harpercollins.co.uk/green.

Printed and bound in Great Britain
by CPI Group (UK) Ltd, Croydon, CR0 4YY

For Karen and Andrea, who brought Triathlon Dad to my attention!

Many thanks to Mary, Geordie, Diane and Michael, who allow us to share the Spanish sunshine with them, and Chellie, who always has my back. xx

CHAPTER ONE

'TRIATHLON DAD IS finally in the building,' Summer muttered under her breath as Dr Rafael Valdez made his way to the day-care centre.

He was still some distance away but she followed his progress along the walkway from the main building and the reactions of the patients and staff of the clinic as they stopped to stare at the handsome Spanish surgeon. It was hard not to, even for someone who'd quit her job at a prominent hospital and come to this island to escape the temptations of handsome men and the chaos they created.

Although only a couple of miles off the coast of Boston, Maple Island gave the impression she was far from the troubles she'd left on the mainland as it was only accessible by ferry or light aircraft. They were still susceptible to the same wintry weather here as the city she'd grown up in at this time of the year, but there was a distinct vacation vibe about this laid-back place that meant it never really bothered her. It wouldn't be long before the sun was shining again and the influx of tourists would double the size of the population. As long as she didn't dabble in any holiday romances, or any romances for that matter, she could live here happily.

Unfortunately, her job as a child-care assistant in the staff nursery meant it wasn't as easy to avoid Dr Valdez as she'd prefer when he was a reminder that, despite her vow, she wasn't immune to handsome men. He was fit in more ways than one with the perfect body to match those dark good looks, honed by all the swimming, running and cycling around the island that had also earned him his sporty nickname. He was a perfect treat for the eyes but that was all he was to Summer, or ever could be. Even if he wasn't a co-worker—she'd learned to avoid them at all costs in romantic notions, since she couldn't keep moving after every failed relationship—he only had eyes for one girl around here.

'It looks as though he has a fight on his hands this morning.' Kaylee, her colleague, had apparently noticed the object of her attention too.

The love of his life, his three-year-old daughter, Graciela, was one of Summer's charges and the reason she got to spend more time with him than was good for her. Regardless of the physical attraction she might harbour towards him, they were often locked in battle over the best way to care for his child's extra needs. There was a personality clash that cancelled out the allure of his outward appearance, even if his single-dad status hadn't already put him at the top of her off-limits list.

The last time she'd lost her heart to a father-and-child combo she'd mistaken her ex's relationship of convenience for love. Whilst she had been throwing herself into that nurturing role to look after his son Leo, thinking it was leading up to a permanent arrangement for them as a family, Marc had been using her as a stop-gap until his baby mama came back on the scene.

She wouldn't make the mistake again of giving her trust, her future, to someone who didn't appreciate her worth beyond her child-minding skills. Since she was already paid to do that for Rafael Valdez, she knew the score. If she let herself get drawn into the middle of another parent-and-child set-up she only had herself to blame this time around.

She watched Gracie turning round and running off in the opposite direction for the umpteenth time, taking them twice as long to reach the nursery than usual. Instead of demonstrating more patience, her father simply swung her up into his arms and marched on despite her protests.

Summer had witnessed her fair share of toddler tantrums but a child on the autism spectrum needed extra-careful handling and would have no concept of making her father late for work at any age.

'Something must've happened this morning to make them late. He hasn't even had time to dry his hair.'

Even from this distance Summer could see his still-wet hair glistening in the sunlight.

That wasn't a big deal in itself, but whatever had caused this disruption to their routine had the potential to become an issue for Gracie. Summer loved working with the little girl but she had communication issues and learning difficulties that often led to these bursts of temper.

She caught sight of Kaylee smirking at her. 'What?'

Okay, so she was imagining Rafael's dark hair curling at the nape of his neck and soaking his collar. It didn't mean anything other than she noticed the small details in other people's lives. People-reading was part of her skill as a child life specialist, even if her job here required more of her child-care services for now.

Alex Kirkland, the medical director and one of the clinic's founders, had employed her with a view to eventually moving her into her preferred position. With the extension of the children's ward in the future she would be needed more in her role as a child life specialist to help the young patients cope with their illnesses and prepare them for whatever medical procedures they faced.

She was happy to wear either hat if she could stay here, leaving the mess of her personal life back in Boston. It wasn't as if she was missed when Marc and Leo were back living as a family with his ex and her own mother had her second husband to support her instead of Summer.

'Nothing,' Kaylee replied, obviously meaning everything as she did a double take between Summer and the two figures she hadn't been able to take her eyes off.

'Oh, shut up!' Summer hit her playfully over the head with a soft-bodied panda she'd been minding for one of the children.

Not for the first time she wondered where the child's mother was, or any other family for that matter. There was very little known about the spinal surgeon other than what a coup it was to have him on board here. Despite his sterling reputation as a surgeon, she'd found him difficult, stubborn and resistant to taking on any friendly advice. If he had that attitude to people other than her it could explain his single status, regardless of him being so smoulderingly attractive. Even she experienced that flutter in the pit of her stomach when he was near. She'd seen how loving he could be with his daughter so she knew there was a soft heart in there somewhere.

It might come across as judgemental but sometimes she thought parents often didn't try hard enough to salvage a relationship when children were involved. Broken families would always be a source of pain to her when they represented her own difficult background. The children suffered most when the parents decided they couldn't live together and, in her case, not only had she lost her father but he'd taken her stepbrother too, severing all contact between them and leaving her feeling incomplete.

Robbie may not have been her biological sibling but she'd grown up thinking of him as her big brother, someone she could turn to for advice or comfort, and losing him had been akin to having a limb cut off. Since then, she'd lived her life always feeling as though something was missing, and the loss of a mother had to be even more devastating to a child of Gracie's young years.

She never talked about her mom and she'd noticed Dr Valdez didn't wear a wedding ring so there didn't appear to be a significant other anywhere in the background. There was a chance he was nursing a broken heart, which would explain his defensive behaviour. It was the same reason Summer had come to Maple Island in much the same mood at first. Perhaps he was finding life as a single dad difficult. Given time, he might get back together with his ex again too, just as Marc had when he'd left Summer out in the cold over a year ago. Apparently, it was easier to share the parenting of a small child with their *actual* parent rather than someone who'd been learning on the job.

Men with motherless children were double heartbreak waiting to happen because when things ended you lost them both. Regardless of the love and time given to help raise their offspring, when the relationship was over an ex-girlfriend didn't have any right to remain in the child's life. Losing Marc had been difficult, but having five-year-old Leo taken away from her too had been devastating when she'd come to think of him as her own. Until Marc had decided to forgive his ex for cheating on him when she'd asked to come back and, just like that, Summer had been surplus to requirements.

That bitter taste of loss and betrayal tinged her objectivity. She knew nothing of the secrets the Valdezes might be hiding and she intended to keep it that way, having sworn not to get involved with another family outside the workplace again. If and when she decided to date again, her requirements for a suitor would include being single with no dependants or exes lurking in the background.

She doubted Rafael had any desire to jump into the dating quagmire either. There certainly hadn't been any talk of him seeing anyone since arriving on the island and his devotion to his patients, including the ten-year-old Walsh twins who'd suffered severe spinal injuries and were taking up a lot of his attention, didn't leave him with much down time.

She might not view him as relationship potential but she could see he was a good father, trying to give his daughter the best start in life and struggling with the demands of juggling his home and work life. It couldn't be easy for a busy single dad contending with the special needs of an autistic daughter and Summer would never dare criticise his parenting skills but it wouldn't hurt him to ask for or accept help once in a while.

Her own mother had been equally as pigheaded when they'd been left as half of a family when her father had taken off, refusing financial or emotional assistance from any quarter. As an adult she recognised how her mother must've been hurting badly to be so determined to do everything on her own and prove she didn't need a man around. Except Summer had been the one to suffer, forced to grow up too quickly and dragged into the conflict between her parents by having to choose which one to live with. She hoped Gracie would never be subjected to that kind of stress when it could have such a devastating impact on her development.

It hadn't been fair to Summer as an eight-year-old to put her under that much pressure to pick sides, but emotions had been running high and she'd been compelled to stay with her mother since her father had been the one having an affair. Once she'd made her position known, her father had demanded custody of her stepbrother and moved abroad to start a new life with the woman he'd left them for.

They'd all been devastated by the split but her parents had wanted a complete separation, things having been said and done that neither could apparently overlook in order to let the siblings maintain contact. Perhaps they'd imagined they had been young enough to forget and would get over it, but she hadn't and now she didn't even know where to start looking for Robbie.

With hindsight she could understand why her mother had chosen never to rely on anyone else after that epic betrayal, but when her health had suffered, Summer had been the only one there to pick up the pieces.

Unable to work full time, there had been no money to fund things every other child took for granted and it hadn't been long before she'd been taking on after-school jobs to supplement their income at a time when her teenage peers had been going to parties or shopping for clothes. She'd never resented her mother for those sacrifices but when she had eventually married again Summer had gone a little wild, exploring her sudden freedom and leaving her responsibilities far behind. They hadn't really been close since. She'd even been replaced at home.

Summer had no wish to interfere in anyone else's life but Dr Valdez didn't have to be Gracie's whole world. There were no parent-of-the-year prizes for running yourself into the ground, only more problems for the child when there was no one else around to lend a helping hand.

She'd studied hard to enable her to work with vulnerable children and she knew how much time and patience it took to communicate effectively to make any progress in their development. If he would simply give her the chance, she was willing to share everything she'd learned to make their lives a little easier.

'Hold this for me,' she said, handing the plush toy to Kaylee, and left her vantage point to meet them in the corridor, persuading herself her actions were based purely on Graciela's needs.

When she reached Rafael, he'd changed tactics and was murmuring in soothing placatory Spanish to his daughter. Summer's school-level Spanish was rusty but she recognised *'Te amo, mija'*, because he told Gracie he loved her each time he had to leave her in child-care to go to work. It melted her heart that he could be so curt with people at times yet wasn't afraid to express his feelings for his daughter. She wouldn't have been human if she didn't wonder what it would be like to have him whisper sweet Spanish nothings into her ear too, or experience the delicious shivers up her neck when she imagined him there.

'I can take her from here if you'd like?' Graciela immediately stopped fidgeting once she took her hand.

It had taken weeks to get her to this stage when she'd screamed the place down every time her father was out of sight at first. There were still problems with those who worked with her on late shifts when Rafael was on nights at the clinic, but she was lucky Gracie responded to her so positively.

'We're fine, thank you,' he insisted, yet as she dropped Graciela's hand, the little one began stamping her feet. The low whimpering in her throat began to build until it would soon become that ear-piercing shriek to let everyone know she wasn't happy. It was difficult for children like Gracie to communicate their needs effectively and the tantrums were often born of frustration.

Summer stood her ground before Rafael's stubborn pride, or lack of faith in her ability to do her job effectively, distressed the child any further.

'If she's happy to come with me now, it means you can get to work quicker.' It was logical to anyone who wasn't a helicopter parent, who didn't trust another soul with the care of their precious offspring, that she was offering him the perfect solution.

'Graciela, would you like to come and have a teddy bears' picnic with us this morning? You can pick any toy you want and we'll spread out the tea set for the party.' Addressing her directly didn't always elicit a response but on this occasion Gracie made her preference known by clinging onto Summer's forearm with both hands. Her triumphant smile was a victory for common sense and a sharp contrast to Rafael's frown, but he didn't try to sway his daughter any further in his direction.

'Here are her things.' Her papa shrugged the sparkly pink backpack down his arms to give it to her. As well as proving how comfortable he was in his own masculinity, the girly, child-sized bag he carried for his daughter emphasised the broadness of his shoulders and gave Summer a temporary moment of fancy. She'd seen his muscles ripple at the swimming pool as they powered him through the water at breakneck speed and could easily imagine the upper-body strength he possessed. One flex and he could probably burst the straps as if they were made of tissue paper.

Simply thinking about that display of machismo awakened her girlish appreciation... and was it hot in here because she was in desperate need of a fan right now? Here was a man so strong in body yet he had no problem setting aside the discomfort many men would've shown with such a small act to make his child feel comfortable in her surroundings. He had a gentle way with his daughter she hadn't fully grasped because he did it in such a quiet way without making a fuss or expecting ebullient praise, like Marc often had.

Perhaps she'd merely convinced herself Rafael had an inflated opinion of himself because she'd pigeonholed him right along with the last single dad she'd known. There was also the possibility she was finding excuses not to like him because she knew she was developing quite a crush.

Summer graciously accepted the handover and did her best to ignore the zing that came from the simple brush of their fingers during the exchange. The increased heart rate and tingling sensation where he'd touched her was nothing more than a sign that she knew she was playing with fire here. She shouldn't be thinking of him as anything other than a parent at the day-care centre but forbidden fruit always seemed that much more tantalising.

'She'll be fine, Dr Valdez.' It was her turn to

dismiss him so she could get on with her job without having him distracting her with his muscles and sexy accent. She might also have to start wearing mittens if she was to prevent herself from going into raptures every time they came into brief physical contact.

He bent down to kiss the top of his daughter's head before walking away.

'Thank you, Miss Ryan.' He tossed a measure of gratitude back over his shoulder. It should have riled her when she was blatantly an afterthought but she drank it in like an eager-to-please lapdog, thirsty for praise. The only consolation she took from being such a slave to her hormones was that this exchange would probably stay with him for the remainder of the day too. If only because he'd been forced to accept her help in some small way.

Just breathe. Rafael did his best to keep walking and ignore the urge to look back. He didn't think he'd be able to handle the sight of his daughter happier to co-operate with a member of staff than with him. The whole attraction of coming to Maple Island Clinic had been the idea of having Graciela close, and though he was relieved she'd stopped her theatrics this morning he hated the idea that someone could do a better job than him of looking after her.

His career was always going to keep him busy but he'd been sold on life here with the excellent child-care facilities Alex Kirkland and Cody Brennan had told him they provided on site when they'd lured him away from Boston Harbour Hospital. Although everything here on Maple Island had lived up to expectations, it hadn't made the separation anxiety any easier. After his wife Christina had walked out on them he'd been doing the job of both parents and he was under pressure not to fail his daughter the way her mother had.

So far, it didn't seem as though he was making a great job of it. Summer made him feel inadequate when it came to looking after his daughter for the simple reason she was doing a better job of it than he was. Regardless of his workload, he always made time for a leisurely breakfast together before he dropped her off at nursery. It was the one meal he was guaranteed to spend with his daughter. He appreciated that quality time together and he was sure that on some level Gracie did too.

Those rare family moments had been few and far between for him as a child. As Spanish nobility, his parents had always had more important business to attend to and had often dined elsewhere or at different times from their children. When they had been at home dinner had become an elaborate affair where he had been preened and polished before being allowed to dine with whatever dignitaries had been in residence. If at all.

It was a small rebellion against that regime by making breakfast a casual occasion, eaten whilst wearing pyjamas and before a hair or a tooth had been brushed, but it was his and Gracie's ritual. He'd slipped up this morning by oversleeping and thinking he could get away with a juice box and a cereal bar on the go. It was never going to be that easy when he'd ripped her from her usual morning routine.

His mistake in sleeping through the alarm had been compounded by having the battle to get Gracie through the nursery door in Summer's presence. It was bad enough leaving other people to do most of the caring for his daughter when he was working, without anyone witnessing his epic parenting fail. Summer in particular was always offering advice on how he could best manage Gracie's challenging behaviour, as though she knew her better than he did.

Okay, she was acting in the best interests of his little girl and on some level he was grateful for the one-on-one attention she was receiving in day-care with regard to her extra needs. However, times such as this succeeded in making him feel guiltier than ever about his workload and the possibility he was neglecting her in any capacity.

It was absurd, of course. Graciela was his life, his reason for being, but he found it difficult to trust again or rely on anyone other than himself to do right by her. Christina's sudden departure had impacted on every area of his life and he'd had to employ the help of his young neighbour, Mags, to babysit whilst he'd tried to make permanent day-care arrangements. They'd used her before without any problems on the rare occasion he and

Christina had gone out as a couple for the evening. One emergency late-night call-out had changed everything.

Although it had been last minute, Mags had agreed to mind Gracie overnight while he went to the hospital to perform emergency surgery on a car-crash victim. He'd thought his daughter would be safe in her own home with someone he knew and trusted. Mags had never offered him a true account or explanation of what had happened that night but from what he'd gathered, the lure of a party in the neighbourhood had proved too great to resist. She'd left Gracie alone and his baby's cries had been heard and reported to the police by other concerned neighbours.

He'd been confronted at work by police and child protection services as though he'd been the one to abandon her. Even when a tearful Mags had confessed what she'd done, Rafael had been subjected to interrogation and suspicion by social workers to the point he'd taken leave from his job to prove his devotion to his daughter.

Eventually he'd had to return and put some

level of faith in agency childminders since they had the relevant checks and qualifications. However, that overwhelming feeling of guilt for what had happened, or what could have happened, had never left him. Even then, he hadn't been able to shake the notion the efficient, professional women who'd enabled him to return hadn't cared for Gracie much beyond their pay checks. Not the way Summer did.

Graciela had flourished since coming to the island and it would take time to come to terms with not being her sole source of support. He was thankful that there was someone who could reach her where others had failed but he was wary of their developing bond. Simply because it was drawing him closer to Summer too and that wasn't somewhere he should be when he was supposed to be concentrating on his daughter.

He'd been hurt too much to risk another entanglement and though his head reminded him of that at every given opportunity, his senses and his body were more easily led astray. It was difficult to keep that security wall in place when Summer kept breaching it with a look or a touch and the sweet scent of her perfume that smelled like candy.

In any other circumstances he would have welcomed someone else's devotion to his daughter but he hadn't let anyone get close to them since his wife had broken their hearts. He'd always been attracted to strong, independent women and Summer wasn't afraid to challenge him when necessary but he would never be distracted again when it came to Gracie's welfare.

The way Summer was already so integrated into their lives was unnerving but Gracie had never responded so well to a female influence. Not even her own mother. Christina had been hurt by her refusal to interact with her at an early age, had taken it personally when it had merely been a symptom of her condition. She'd been embarrassed when their baby had failed to reach the milestones of others her age. In the end she'd simply told Rafael she wasn't cut out for motherhood or marriage and had gone back to the single, carefree life she'd apparently missed so much.

The irony was that he'd been able to get the

help and advice needed to aid Gracie after she'd gone. Christina had been in denial that her baby could be anything other than perfect, when Rafael had known all along there had been something wrong. Once he'd been able to get a diagnosis so they knew what they were dealing with, it had been easier to cope. If Christina had hung around she would've watched her child reach all those milestones, if slightly later than her peers.

It hadn't made life as a single parent any easier to have a daughter with special needs and there certainly wasn't room for a Christina replacement. He couldn't trust anyone not to hurt Gracie again.

Miss Ryan had to remain a mere bystander when it came to his family. Otherwise he was doomed to repeat the past and the opportunity to come to Maple Island would have been wasted. He hadn't relocated here for anything other than the stability it offered Gracie. Bringing another woman into their home wasn't going to achieve that, only offer more possibilities of heartache when she decided

Gracie was too much reality for a pretty young blonde to handle.

Rafael had had his time of putting his wants first when he'd left his family behind in Spain to come and study medicine in America. Unlike his parents, he wanted what was best for his child, not necessarily what was more acceptable for them. That selfishness and all the other negative family connotations he'd turned his back on could stay in the Mediterranean as far as he was concerned.

Rafael's mood hadn't improved at all by the afternoon. As usual he'd had a busy morning catching up on the day's schedule, meeting the team at the facility to discuss the status of their patients and prioritise his cases depending on the urgency of their conditions.

One of the reasons he'd relocated to the clinic had been the hope it would be less demanding on his time, making more room for Gracie, with fewer emergencies coming in at all hours of the night when they were primarily a rehabilitation facility.

However, his caseload was always full, dealing with back-related conditions that required surgical intervention. The clinic's reputation, combined with the privacy and beautiful surroundings provided by the location, made it the ideal hiding place for the rich and famous wishing to recuperate away from the glare of the spotlight and the paparazzi.

He understood that mind-set to some extent. Unknown to his fellow islanders, he was a bit of a celebrity in his own right. In Spain, at least. The eldest son of a duke attracted more attention than he'd ever been comfortable with, and though he'd been glad to leave that cosseted lifestyle behind to come to America and study anonymously, it had caused a huge fallout with his family, but he didn't regret the sacrifice he'd made when it meant he and Gracie retained their privacy.

The majority of Rafael's clients here tended to be sports stars keen to recover from injury as quickly and quietly as possible and the on-site rehab facilities provided everything they needed post-surgery.

He didn't follow American sports himself but even he'd heard of Tom Horner, the ex-football star turned commentator, who was here for a lumbar discectomy to relieve his sciatica pain. The procedure Rafael was carrying out today was to remove the herniated portion of the lumbar disc pressing against a nerve.

'*Buenos días*, Doc.' The All-American hero slapped his meaty hand into Rafael's and shook it vigorously. Even now, in his fifties, the man was a powerhouse, the strength of the handshake alone reverberating through Rafael's limbs so he dreaded to imagine how much damage a hit from him in his heyday would have caused.

'*Buenas tardes, Señor Horner.* Are you all set for your surgery today?' The surgery unit was still in its infancy at present but sufficient that they could carry out procedures on an outpatient basis. Any major operations were still carried out at their sister hospital, Boston Harbour, and patients were often transferred here for secondary surgeries as well as rehabilitation. Sometimes they had a team out from Boston to assist and other times Rafael's expertise was required back on the mainland

and the sharing of skills was working success-fully so far.

'I can't wait to have it done and get back to normal.' From his appearance alone no one would be able to tell this man had been in pain for some considerable time. A lot of people tended to look vulnerable sitting in a hospital bed in their gowns, waiting to put their lives literally in the hands of the doctors here. Not Tom Horner. His hulking frame dominated the space, the fabric of the flimsy gown stretched to accommodate him and he was as intimidat-ing a presence as ever.

'You know you'll have to take it easy for a while after surgery? We'll discuss it at length post-op but we need to make sure you avoid any undue strain to keep your spine in proper alignment.' He knew Tom's kind, having started out in sports therapy. Sportsmen didn't make the easiest patients, wanting to shake off injury as soon as possible to get back on their feet and back in the game, often ignoring rehab advice to their detriment.

'Don't worry, Doc. I've hired a place on the west side of the island where I'm doing nothing but resting up until I'm fighting fit again. As far as anyone knows, I'm on extended vacation and I want to keep it that way.'

'Of course.' Although wear and tear on the body was all part of the ageing process, Rafael had treated men and women who saw it as a sign of weakness, almost something to be ashamed about. Whilst it wasn't his business who his patients did or didn't tell about their health problems, it was his duty to ensure there was some after-care in place at home. 'Do you have any family or friends over with you who can help you out during your recuperation?'

He hadn't seen any evidence of a support system even at the initial consultation in Boston before Tom had followed him out here, over the moon at the prospect of having his treatment in private.

The big man's cheeks turned pink before he answered. 'My daughter's here, fussing around. She insisted on coming with me but as far as the ex-wife is concerned we're on a father-daughter getaway. Terri can read me better than her mom ever could and knew there was something going on.' He threw his hands up in exasperation and the fact his daughter had got the better of him made the corners of Rafael's mouth tilt upwards for the first time that day.

Daughters had that knack of tying their fathers up in knots around their little fingers. Thankfully that bond didn't break even when the marriage did. At least, not for him. Gracie's mother hadn't had any problem abandoning her child but she'd never taken to being a parent the way he had and now he was doing the job for both of them.

The responsibility of motherhood had curbed her nights out when he'd been working and unable to mind their daughter. A baby with special needs had been a step too far for a woman who had still thought and acted like a single twenty-something. It had almost been a relief when she'd ended things because they'd been able to stop pretending she was a wife or a mother. It was entirely Christina's loss she'd never got to be part of her beautiful daughter's life, the daughter who'd exceeded all of those damning predictions regarding her development.

He'd made a success of his life without the assistance of his family and at least Gracie had a father who loved her and would do everything he could to ensure she thrived.

'I'm glad you have someone to make sure you do as you're told. It will help your recovery.' The clinic staff would operate, provide medication and follow-up treatment, including physiotherapy, but there were practical things Tom would require at home to smooth the transition from the clinic.

'Don't worry, Terri's at the beach house now, adapting it for the return of the invalid. She even insisted on buying me slip-on loafers for the duration of my stay so I don't have to bend down to tie my laces.' The absolute horror on his face that he should be subjected to such an atrocity was comical. Rafael silently wished Terri good luck, hoping she would prove equally as stubborn as her father. She'd probably have to tie him down to prevent him from rushing his recovery.

'Think yourself fortunate to have someone willing to take care of you. Not everyone does.' He had a momentary lapse into self-pity, considering his options should he ever find himself in the same situation. There were no loving family members around for him to rely on. It was a sobering and ironic thought that he'd probably have to pay someone to provide that assistance.

If he'd stayed in San Sebastian, as his parents had wanted, and had never left Spain, he would've had every medical or child expert available to the eldest son of a duke. Therein had lain the problem. He'd never wanted to remain tied to that lifestyle, living off ancient connections to the royal family and trying to stay relevant by portraying himself like his playboy brother to the paparazzi.

This life of anonymity had suited him better, even though his family had seen his move to the States as a betrayal of his heritage. He hadn't spoken to them since but as they hadn't accepted him for who he was, he knew they would never acknowledge Gracie for being different either. She wouldn't fit into the perfect family they preferred to parade for the cameras, neither would he subject her to those expectations.

He had played along for a while for appearances' sake but Gracie wouldn't understand that's what she was supposed to do and she shouldn't have to pretend to be someone she wasn't. It was better for her to be loved for who she was, even if he was the only one in her life able to give her that unconditional love.

Unfortunately, that left him with no next of kin here if anything should happen to him. Tom should appreciate someone caring enough not to back away when he needed them most.

'Not as fortunate as you, Doc, that's for sure. Oo-ee!' Tom's appreciative whistle was lost on Rafael.

'Excuse me?' He cocked his head to one side, waiting for an explanation when he could see no reason why a successful pundit would exhibit the slightest bit of jealousy towards him.

'Forgive me for speaking out of turn but if I had a wife who looked like yours, she wouldn't be an ex.' The bawdy laugh didn't help unravel the mystery for Rafael, only deepened it. He had no idea how anyone here would know about Christina, but if they were acquainted with her they'd also be aware nursing anyone wasn't in her DNA. Her job was strictly in medical research and she wasn't hands on in any way unless she was in a club with her girl-friends in the early hours of the morning and looking for some male attention.

'I think you must be mistaking me for some-one else.' He decided not to go down that dark alley and dismissed it to concentrate on Tom's notes.

Unfortunately, Tom wasn't so easily deterred from whatever it was he thought was going on in Rafael's life.

'I saw you this morning with your family when I came in. Beautiful. You're a very lucky man. We weren't good together, me and Jess, but I miss having that closeness with some-one, you know?'

He didn't know, staring at him blankly for some time before it dawned on him who his patient was referring to.

'Oh. Oh!' An image of him handing over the care of his daughter to Summer in the corri-dor popped into his head. He supposed to an outsider the mistake was understandable but it did knock the breath out of him that Tom had assumed her to be his wife and Gracie's mother. Did she really appear so comfortable in either role?

'Summer's not my wife, she's—' What exactly was she? An employee? A co-worker? None of those titles accurately depicted how significant she'd become in their daily lives yet he couldn't describe her as a friend either. Not when he was trying so hard to resist having her play a part in his personal life for his own sanity.

There was no discernible line between work and personal matters when Summer's efforts with his daughter broke through any perceived barriers. He reaped the benefits at home with Gracie's improved verbal and motor skills apparently honed by the time and energy Summer had put into working with Gracie.

However, with every achievement she accomplished, guilt took a bigger nibble at his conscience—that if he'd spent that time with her instead he could've been the one to further her progress. Except that would have prohibited them from moving to the island, having an income or helping countless people with his surgical skills.

He had to accept some things were out of his control. Including thoughts about Miss Summer Ryan, which seemed to be coming much more frequently and less about educational matters.

Contemplation about her current relationship status, how she was spending her evenings or if she liked him beyond her official capacity were not things he should be concerning himself with if he considered her only in her role at the day-care centre.

He wanted to get to know her but with that came a whole web of complications he couldn't afford to get caught up in again. Investing emotionally in someone other than his daughter left him vulnerable to another rejection or worse, more heartbreak he could do without when he would still have to get up every morning and carry on for Gracie's sake.

'Summer's my daughter's nursery teacher,' he filled in, unwilling to give his patient any further insight into his complicated personal matters. 'Now, are you clear about what's going to happen today in surgery?'

'Could you run it by me again, Doc?'

'I'm going to make a small incision in your lower back and insert a small tube that will act as a corridor for me to access the herniated disc with minimal tissue disruption to the surrounding area. We'll use local anaesthetic and some mild sedation so you won't feel anything.' Sometimes there could be irritation afterwards caused by the operation itself but once the bone spur or disc material causing the pain was removed, patients usually felt an improvement.

'That's all I need to hear.'

'I'm sure we'll have you back on the football field in no time at all.' He closed Tom's file with a smile and tucked it under his arm.

'I spend more time behind the sports desk these days but I appreciate the confidence.'

They parted on a friendly, firm handshake but the exchange had shaken Rafael. It wasn't the fact someone had assumed Summer was part of his family that bothered him. No, it was that the idea wasn't totally unappealing to him. Exactly why he should try extra-hard to push her out and prevent her from doing to him what every other person close to him had done and let him go without a fight.

CHAPTER TWO

'SEE YOU TOMORROW.' Summer waved off another of the little ones for the day as her parents finished work and came to collect their baby.

People came and went from the nursery at different times according to shift patterns or unforeseen overtime. The clinic even provided a live-in night service for those hard-working doctors and nurses who had to cover nights in the clinic and required extra child care. The set-up was all to keep disruption to a minimum for the families of the employees here, and attracted the best medics in their field for that reason.

The day-care aspect of her job could be seen as a step down on the career ladder when she was a highly qualified child life specialist. However, the position she'd held in Boston had proved difficult to transfer from when it was in such a competitive field and she'd needed something, anything, to get her away from her ex-boyfriend and the wife he'd reconciled with.

It had turned out her skills had become useful for the small children's wing they'd later opened at the clinic. Although there wasn't yet a need for a full-time child life specialist, she'd come to an arrangement with Alex and Cody to go wherever she was needed most.

Currently, she was content to help keep the children entertained at day-care but the arrival of the Walsh twins on the island had ensured her diary was full in both areas.

'Papa?' At the sign of activity around the door, Gracie came to stand beside her with her pink backpack clutched in her hands.

'Not yet, Gracie. Your papa was working very hard today so he might be a bit later than usual.' The erratic hours were something the staff accounted for but it could be difficult for the children to comprehend. Especially for the younger ones or those like Gracie with learning difficulties. It didn't matter how often she was told her father wouldn't be taking her home yet, when she saw other parents arriving for their sons and daughters she expected to leave with them. The best thing in these circumstances was to try and distract her until Rafael did get here.

'Home.'

'I know you want to go home, sweetheart. Why don't we make your papa a nice picture while we're waiting?' Summer eased the bag out of her hands and hung it back on her coat peg. With the aid of some glitter and glue she could try and keep her busy enough to forget his absence temporarily.

Summer wasn't privy to the family circumstances but from observation she could see life wasn't easy for father or daughter without the mother's presence. What Gracie needed more than anyone or anything was stability and currently the sea of ever-changing faces managing her care was doing nothing to aid that.

There was no one nominated care-giver at present, with different staff managing her needs according to the rotas and time sheets. The attention Summer provided whenever she could seemed to calm Gracie down, the meltdowns less frequent during her shifts. Perhaps it was because Gracie trusted her, or that she took more time trying to understand her than the staff who might not have as much as experience with special needs children, but she responded to Summer. Sometimes.

Without speaking or making eye contact, Gracie put a purple crayon into her hand and in her own way indicated she was supposed to contribute to the picture too. Summer pulled up one of the tiny chairs to join her at the colouring table.

'You want me to do something?'

'Draw,' Gracie demanded, tapping the page impatiently.

With confident strokes Summer drew the bold outline of a flower, which her co-artist set about obliterating with a succession of colourful scribbles. She didn't mind staying on even when her working day had supposedly ended. It wasn't as though she had anyone waiting for her at home, or anything of a social life that necessitated consideration.

The child's learning difficulties would probably require extra assistance when she reached school age but for now Summer was of the opinion she was the most qualified person in the nursery to look after her. There was no formal arrangement in place but if Rafael, the day-care manager and the medical directors agreed, she wanted to put herself forward to care exclusively for Gracie. Outside her clinic responsibilities, of course. That way there wouldn't be a stream of strangers coming into her life day and night when Summer was willing to be there for her every minute she could, and offer that stability Gracie was lacking.

The biggest obstacle to overcome in that plan would be Dr Valdez himself and his insistence he could do everything single-handedly. If this morning was any indication, he was resistant to any offer of help. He'd been so defensive about the idea of her accompanying Gracie to nursery for him one would've thought she'd come from child protective services to take her from him permanently, not do him a favour.

'Your father's going to love this.'

Gracie smeared glue and glitter in between the now indistinguishable petals, turning the flower into a sparkly, purple blob she was sure the proud daddy would display along with her other works of art.

There was no verbal response from her protégé but once Gracie was interested in something it often became her sole focus. Although that could be problematic in public places, it did prove useful when Summer had to go elsewhere. Like now, as she saw Rafael through the window, striding towards the nursery unit.

She wanted to intercept him before Gracie spotted him and shut down any chance of a private talk about future arrangements for his daughter.

'Kaylee, could you watch Gracie for a minute while I talk to her father?' Summer quietly caught the attention of her colleague, trying not to disturb her art student or alert her to her father's appearance in the process.

'Sure.' Quickly and quietly, Kaylee slid into the seat she'd vacated and Summer hoped she could achieve her goal before the switch became apparent.

With ninja-like stealth she slipped out, closed the door gently behind her and managed to accost her target in the hallway.

'Dr Valdez, could I have a word with you about Graciela?' She positioned herself directly in front of him, forcing him to come to a halt.

'I'm late. Sorry.' He rubbed his hands over his face, giving her some indication of the day he'd had. His dark brown eyes were hooded and heavy as though he hadn't slept well in days and it made her more determined to offer some assistance. She wasn't sure the man knew how to relax but she'd been around enough children with special medical needs to understand the toll it could take on the parents without them realising the importance of self-care.

There was also her experience of watching her own mom's health decline rather than accept outside help. All those years of hard manual work her mother had done to earn a living, taking on cleaning jobs where she could, had caused the early onset of arthritis and limited her mobility at a relatively early age. If they'd given in and let someone else into their circle of trust, that might've been prevented, or at least delayed.

Summer opened her mouth to assure him

she wasn't here to scold him or delay him any longer than necessary, only for him to dodge around her. She backed up, praying there was nothing in her path she could fall over as she tottered backwards, trying to keep up with him. In the end she resorted to grabbing his arm to get him to stop, almost knocked completely off balance by the discovery of the taut muscles beneath his pale blue shirt.

It must be the swimming, she mused, before her mind drifted towards his cycling and running regime and what effect that might have on other parts of his body.

She shouldn't be thinking of him in such a fashion but her imagination seemed to run wild where Rafael was concerned. Not only was it a conflict of interest when he was the parent of one of the children she worked alongside, but he represented everything she was afraid of in a potential partner. He had a young child she was already attached to, and they worked at the same clinic so any romantic daydreaming about him was a disaster waiting to happen.

By blurring that line she would put her job and her heart in jeopardy. She was afraid she mightn't have any choice in the matter when she was fixating on something as innocent as touching his arm and reacting as though he'd given her a lap dance.

Rafael stared at the hand on his arm, then at her, his eyebrows raised at her audacity. She had to fight through the foggy muddle of her brain now flicking through snapshots of him in cycle shorts and sweat-drenched running gear to search for words to string a sentence together. Perhaps she really should think about getting back into the dating scene—restricted to single men she didn't work with—if her body was so desperately craving some inter-action with male company.

'Gracie. There should be a constant in her life.' It didn't quite articulate everything she'd intended but it was the gist of why she'd come out here to him and sufficient for that dark scowl to slide over his face as he began walk-ing away again.

'I was in surgery. It couldn't be helped. I'll collect her now and we'll be on our way.'

No, no, no. This wasn't going the way she'd

planned at all. She'd merely succeeded in ticking him off even more.

She spun around and was forced into a half-run to catch up with him this time.

'Can you stop so we can talk properly?' Okay, she was verging on the bossy side of insolence in a professional capacity but the man was infuriating at times.

He pulled on the brakes with a hiss of air through his teeth. 'What exactly is it you want, Miss Ryan?'

Miss Ryan. Not Summer, as every other person on the island referred to her. She was sure he did it to annoy her, keeping things formal so it was impossible for her to penetrate his defences.

'Sorry, I wasn't criticising you. What I meant to say was that I'd like to offer some assistance with Gracie's care. I thought I might take on sole responsibility for her nursery care where I can. I'd have to run it past my superiors but I think that continuity of care when you're working would help her flourish. You saw yourself how stressed she gets with change.'

* * *

'This is about us running late this morning?' He shook his head, any possibility of him agreeing to her plans evaporating before her eyes.

'No.' She refused to be embarrassed about standing up for what she believed in, although her temple was throbbing with the threat of a stress headache. This was so much harder than it ought to be and he was making it that way. Or it could be her recent inability to express herself adequately. Something she'd never had trouble with previously.

If it wasn't for their common goal of getting Gracie as settled into island life as possible she'd have given up explaining herself and gone home for date night with a tub of mint choc chip. Unfortunately, that wasn't going to help anyone and would only make her feel even more nauseous than she was for having started this conversation in the first place.

She took a deep breath and cleared her mind of everything except the little dark-haired girl who lived predominantly in a world of her own and started over. 'As you're aware, I have experience of dealing with children who have specific needs and I was merely suggesting we could discuss an arrangement for Gracie. I would have no objection to taking over her care, day or night, if it suited you, rather than having a variety of new faces parading through her life.'

He studied her silently for a moment too long, those dark eyes scrutinising her every word and body language as though searching for her true intentions. Well, he had nothing to fear. As far as she was concerned, it was about time someone else stood up for Gracie along with her father.

Finally, he said, 'I don't think so,' and left so abruptly Summer gasped at his brusque dismissal. No discussion. No explanation. No gratitude. She was sorry she'd even approached him about the matter when she didn't appear to be anything more than a nuisance to the busy surgeon.

Rafael didn't stop to hear any more or break into a smile until he walked into the nursery unit where he was assaulted in the face with his daughter's painting. Summer reached them as they were preparing to leave, no further conversation apparently warranted as he took his daughter's hand.

'*Vámonos*, Graciela.'

Let's go. He may as well have added they needed to get away from this crazy lady by the way he was staring at her. As he swung the child up onto his shoulders and walked away, singing to her in that deep Spanish burr, Summer wondered if he had a split personality or simply a Summer Ryan aversion when he was so wonderful with his daughter and his patients.

Her sigh was full of regret for the tunnel vision he had when it came to Gracie's guardianship but also because, no matter how she tried, she couldn't get Rafael to like her. Although extremely rare, it was still soul-destroying when issues occurred between her and parents of the children she worked with. This was worse, when lusting after him wasn't something they could easily work through together. The best that she could hope for was that he'd learn to tolerate her for Gracie's sake and she'd get over this crush, soon, before it began to affect more than her concentration.

Supper. Bath. Bed. It was a routine Rafael had been able to implement with Gracie from an early age and had been working very effectively. Until now.

'Come on, Gracie. We're both tired. Why don't you put your pyjamas on and I'll read you a story in bed?' He'd given up on the other two stages now when the walls were coated in the supper he'd made and he was soaked from head to toe with bath water while Gracie remained bone dry.

'No.' She ran off again down the hall away from all thoughts of sleep when it was all he wanted to do.

He pulled the plug out of the bath and drained away what water there was left in the tub and used a towel to mop up the rest on the floor. She'd got into the bath initially but, rather than sit down and play with her toys as usual, she'd stood screaming and kicking the water until he'd had no option but to lift her out again.

Rafael couldn't stand to see her distressed yet he didn't know what had set her off tonight.

'*Por favor.* Please, Gracie.' The toddler pulled off her bath robe and streaked away from him, screeching at the top of her lungs.

At the lowest point of his day now, he was tempted to reconsider Summer's proposal. If he withdrew the inference that he wasn't being a good enough parent to manage alone, he still didn't think it a good idea to turn over responsibility of Gracie's care to someone else merely on their say-so.

Once the red mist had dissipated he could see Summer had meant well and he should've been more appreciative of her interest, more gracious in his refusal of the offer. After all she had nothing to gain in making herself available for Gracie except, in his mind, the possibility of undermining his position in his daughter's life and taking the moral high ground. He knew it was a ridiculous notion but he was so unaccustomed to having people help it made him wary.

The last time he'd felt backed into a corner, forced to ask someone else to share the responsibility, he'd almost lost his daughter and had had his commitment to her questioned. It wasn't easy for him to swallow his pride and his fears and accept genuine support when it was being given freely.

If Summer could see the two of them now she'd be entitled to wag a finger and say, 'See? You need me,' before providing the calm voice of reason his daughter might be more inclined to listen to than her father. He'd worked alongside Summer enough in the clinic with the twins to have experienced that patience she had with the children and the rapport she was able to build with them individually. It was the same with Gracie.

If he was honest about why he didn't want her involved in his life beyond the clinic, it was that building panic at the thought of letting her get too close to his daughter, or him, on a personal level. She had a sweet smile to match her easygoing nature around the kids and it was impossible not to be impressed by her dedication as well as her beauty, but he hadn't moved to an island to find himself in exactly the same situation he'd left in Boston.

He couldn't afford to start relying on her being there for him in case the time came when she decided she'd had enough too. Then he'd end up back at square one, having to fight through his own grief to support Gracie on his own. It had taken this long to get where they were and now they were happy he had no desire to get knocked back down.

They'd been through too much to have to face that kind of devastation again. Unless he was guaranteed to have a partner willing to be by his side for the rest of his days it was pointless even forming an attachment. Eventually even this beautiful young woman would tire of their demands on her time and want to move on.

Too bad that self-preservation seemed to manifest in his grouchy alter ego intent on protecting him from Summer's charms. His attempt to keep her at arm's length simply seemed to spur her on to display a dogged determination and passion that did nothing to diminish his admiration for her, even though he couldn't show it. He had enough on his hands trying to wrangle a three-year-old to bed without debating the pros and cons of getting into another relationship. There simply wasn't room for another female whirlwind to wreak havoc in his life.

'Graciela Valdez, will you please come here and put your pyjamas on now?' It was half command, half plea. He was willing to forget the last few hours of Gracie Armageddon if she would get into bed and finally go to sleep. Then he might get an hour or two to wind down before he had to do this all over again. Obviously, he needed to retire earlier than he had last night to avoid oversleeping again, when they were still experiencing the effects of that slip-up now.

He'd known Summer's assessment was correct about the disruption to Gracie's routine setting her off on the subsequent trail of mayhem and chaos. Sometimes it was easy to forget this cute bundle couldn't be railroaded into things she didn't want to do for convenience's sake. Logic didn't fit into her life the way it did for most.

He heard the handle turning on Gracie's bedroom door before she emerged, dressed, if not in the night-time attire he'd have chosen for her.

'That's what you're wearing to bed?' He was resigned to letting her wear the colourful mismatched socks, the princess dress he'd bought for her birthday—complete with sparkly tiara—and fairy wings, regardless of how uncomfortable he imagined they'd be to sleep in. If he could get her to sleep there was a chance he could slip the tiara and wings off at some point without causing too much of a fuss. At this point in time he'd agree to wearing a matching outfit if they could just bring this day to an end.

Gracie nodded, her lips pursed and brow furrowed as though she was prepared to fight some more for her fashion choices. Any such notion of another battle of wills left him feeling drained. 'Okay then.'

Except she still had no intention of going to bed as she bounced her way down the staircase to the lounge. Rafael had no option left than to leave her to tire herself out. He knew when to pick his battles with her and this wasn't worth the fight. At least the screaming had stopped and he decided if he wasn't permitted some time to sit back and chill, he may as well catch up on some paperwork. That was the part of his job he wasn't enamoured with and if he completed it during working hours, he'd never have a minute to see his patients.

He let the television babysit his daughter for a few minutes to retrieve the briefcase he'd left in the hall beside his bike, thinking he wouldn't see either again until the next morning. With Gracie sitting happily on the couch, legs swinging and humming along to whatever bright, noisy children's show she'd found, he seated himself at the dining table. It gave him sufficient room to spread out his notes and files and the open-plan style of the villa provided an unobscured view of his daughter at the same time. Although he would have to try and block out the noise or he'd never be able to concentrate.

He set the case on the table and flicked open

the catches. The picture Gracie had presented him with at day-care was laid on top and he set it to one side to stick on the fridge door later, if he could find a space alongside her other artwork. He also lifted out an uneaten orange and a banana beginning to turn brown, leftovers from the lunch he hadn't had time to eat. His pen, his diary and various pieces of stationery lined the bottom of the bag but there were no case notes.

'Where are they?' he asked aloud to the now-empty elaborate lunch pail. His hand connected to his forehead in a slap of sudden realisation. The files were sitting on his desk at work. He'd intended to go back and fetch them from the office but he'd been so preoccupied with picking Gracie up from day-care he'd forgotten. The perfect day from hell.

They lived so close to the clinic it seemed silly not to simply swing by and pick them up, and another glance at Gracie, who was now jumping on the couch, confirmed there was no danger of her going to bed soon. If he could wrestle a coat on her she could accompany him and they'd be there and back in fifteen minutes, tops.

'Hey, Gracie, do you want to come with Papa to work?'

It should've been a quick trip in and out but he hadn't factored in the time spent chatting to passers-by enchanted by his daughter's quirky sense of style.

'Yes, she is quite a character.'

'No, I didn't dress her, this is all her own creation.'

An elderly woman being wheeled through towards the rehab ward hailed the porter to stop as though he was her personal chauffeur. This had to be the infamous Philomena Kerridge-Bates he'd heard was here to recuperate after a broken hip. No one other than a millionairess and a Society Grand Dame would have accessorised her hospital gown with matching priceless diamond earrings and necklace. 'This child should be in bed,' she decreed with a dismissive wave of her elegant hand.

'I agree, she should.' He didn't bother to argue or explain and hold them all up.

Everyone always wanted to offer him parenting advice so he'd become accustomed to it. The sight of a single dad drew pity from all corners, as though he was out of his depth without the child's mother in tow. Strangers weren't aware he'd been her only source of stability and love since birth and they'd been doing fine on their own since Christina had left. They'd probably been better off without her. Just as he was, without parents disappointed in who he'd become because he hadn't fitted in with their idea of how a son should behave and had wanted to earn a living in his own right. Away from family influences and the glare of the spotlight they were happy to live in.

Generally, people on Maple Island had good intentions so he didn't let it get to him and responded to comments with a forced smile. His private life, including his daughter's welfare and his wife's whereabouts, was his business and as such he refused to give anyone the satisfaction of dispelling rumour with fact.

He simply wished Philomena well on her way and reckoned their other feisty resident

Theodore Harrington, or Old Salty as he was better known, might have met his match. The cantankerous fisherman was still recovering after his leg had been crushed when the ferry carrying twins on their way to the clinic had broken down in last month's storms and he'd gone to rescue them.

He'd already been discharged once, but he hadn't looked after himself properly and had ended up badly aggravating the injury. In serious pain again, he'd reluctantly allowed himself to be persuaded to return to the clinic for a longer stretch of rehab, so they could keep an eye on him until he was fully healed.

He wasn't an easy patient to deal with, obviously used to living on his own, but he was now the local hero so they were forced to put up with him and his pearls of wisdom as he told everyone how to do their jobs.

The main problem with the attention Gracie was drawing tonight was that she hated it. She barely tolerated people she knew but strangers were a complete no-go area for her. Anything new and unfamiliar was a source of stress and could easily increase her anxiety level but she knew the clinic and he hadn't imagined there'd be as many people about at this time of night.

In the end he resorted to carrying her to stop the onslaught of head-patting and attempted hugs threatening to trigger his daughter into the mother of all meltdowns.

'We really should be going.' He excused himself from the latest admirer, a sweet old lady who had nothing but compliments about Gracie's big brown eyes, which, yes, were just like her father's. That prompted his koala kid to cling onto his shoulder with her fingernails digging into his skin, head buried in his neck so no one else could see her eyes.

'Sweetheart, I'm going to have to set you down until I find what I'm looking for.' Once they were safely behind the closed door of his office he thought he'd be able to prise her off but she was steadfast. His little girl was nothing if not stubborn. Rafael had no idea where that trait had come from at all and he resented any suggestion he should be the genetic culprit simply because he preferred to do things his own way too.

'No!' Gracie literally dug her heels in, right into his side.

'There's no one else here. Just you and me. See?' He prised her head from his shoulder to show her they were safe and alone in the small room and she relaxed her grip slightly.

Taking advantage of the brief reprieve, he disentangled her and set her down in his leather office chair, despite her protests.

'Hold on tight and I'll take you for a spin.' He did his best to make this fun for her, spinning her around the floor with one hand while the rest of his attention was focused on sorting through the stack of papers on his desk.

'More.' It didn't take long for Gracie to develop a love for the new game.

'*Uno momento*, Graciela.' He turned his back for a second to locate the file he needed.

'Papa!' Gracie screamed for him and he saw her spill out of the chair onto the hard floor a fraction too late to do anything about it. She'd managed to stand up on the seat without him seeing and had lost her balance in the process.

'Graciela! *Lo siento*.' Paperwork abandoned, he rushed to lift the chair, which now had her pinned to the floor, her feet twisted up beneath the seat. His heart was in his mouth, waiting to uncover whatever damage had been caused to her in a moment of distraction.

He held his breath, listening for any sound to give him a sign she was all right. He'd never known her to be this quiet. Then she let out a sob so he could breathe again. He moved the chair aside and set her gently onto his desk. 'Where does it hurt?'

She was wailing too loudly now to answer, or even hear him. He sat her on the edge of his desk, careful not to take his eyes, or hands, off her for a second and checked her all over.

He cupped her head in his hands—she was alert but there was a lump forming at her temple. Her arms and fingers were fine as he could manipulate them, with no sign of broken bones, but she let out a howl as he did the same with her feet. It was her right foot, he soon discovered, that was the source of her pain. As he carefully removed her shoe and pulled off her bright pink sock, he could see the ankle was badly swollen already.

Guilt bubbled in his gut. If only he'd jumped

off his high horse for fifteen minutes and accepted some help to look after her, this might have been avoided. Now, because of his stubbornness, there was a chance she could have done some real damage to herself. The only consolation was that they were in the right place for immediate treatment and he wasted no time in rushing her straight to the emergency department.

While he was there he'd get them to extract the chip from his shoulder so he could start to trust those who genuinely wanted to help him when he clearly didn't always know best.

CHAPTER THREE

THE TERSE EXCHANGE with Rafael earlier had unsettled Summer; it worried her that she'd overstepped the mark and what the consequences could be if he made a formal complaint. He was a highly respected surgeon and she was dispensable in comparison.

The restlessness had sent her out for a walk to clear her head and remind herself how lucky she was to be on the island. It was safe enough here that a woman could go for a stroll along the beach alone at night and not be concerned about potential predators, the way she'd had to do in the city. Crime was practically non-existent here, making it part of the appeal of living on Maple Island. Everyone looked out for each other and she reckoned Sheriff Brady had one of the most coveted jobs on the force.

The only trouble they generally encountered

was with over-exuberant tourists during the summer season. Here she was free to do as she pleased and sometimes she tended to get carried away by that novelty.

Gracie wasn't her daughter and, really, she had no business interfering in how she was raised.

Suddenly, she heard a scream from somewhere up in the rocky outcrop leading down to the sea. She ran towards the sound to find a sobbing mother and a shell-shocked father trying to soothe their son, who was lying spread-eagled on the sand, clearly having taken a fall from a considerable height.

Summer immediately swung into action and called for an ambulance before kneeling beside the boy and his parents. 'Hi, I'm Summer. I work over at the clinic. What's his name?'

'Ben. He just slipped… The rocks must've been wet… There was nothing we could do to catch him.' Clearly struggling with guilt, the father took off his jacket and covered his son as best he could.

'The clinic isn't too far from here and I've called for an ambulance. Help is on the way,'

Summer assured them, although it was apparent they were dealing with a compound fracture that would require surgery as part of his femur was sticking out through the skin on his thigh. A splint simply wouldn't be adequate in this case. It was just as well she wasn't squeamish, having spent most of her working life around the sick and injured. Thankfully he would be given pain relief by the paramedics to cope until the bones were put back into alignment.

'Should we try and move him? It doesn't seem right to leave him lying here on the cold ground.' The mother's instinct to get him somewhere warm was understandable but Summer didn't want to exacerbate the injury any further.

'We might hurt him more by trying to lift him. Leave it to the paramedics, they'll be here shortly and will give him some pain relief before they attempt to move him.'

Although Summer deferred to the first responders when they arrived shortly after, she did accompany them to the emergency room. Not only because the parents had been so shaken up but also because she had nowhere else to be. The accident had taken her mind off Marc, Leo and the reasons why she should continue to stay clear of single dads and their adorable children.

She'd been treated as an afterthought for most of her life, her parents never having taken her wants and needs into consideration before their own, and then Marc, who had rejected her in favour of his ex. Time and again those she'd loved had been taken from her without a thought given to how that loss would affect her. After Robbie and Leo, she couldn't face the heartache again. Her days would be better spent at the hospital, where she could make a difference, rather than mooning over someone she couldn't, and shouldn't, have.

There was some trouble in the hospital when Ben fought the nurses trying to fit an oxygen mask over his face to help him breathe and relax, obviously finding the whole experience overwhelming.

'Ben, the doctors will need to take you to

Theatre to fix that leg for you. They're not trying to hurt you, just help.'

'Will I see the bone? Will I feel them moving it?' His bloodshot eyes were wide with horror.

Summer shook her head and showed him the oxygen mask. 'They'll put a mask like this one around your mouth and nose. You'll fall asleep and when it's all over they'll wake you up again.'

'I'm scared,' he admitted, fat tears rolling down his cheeks.

'There's no need to be afraid. Your parents can go down to Theatre with you if you like and be there when you wake up again. Now, we want you nice and comfortable before we get you to Theatre. This mask will help you breathe in some medicine to make you feel better.' Summer placed the mask over his face but the boy wasn't convinced, turning his head away.

She pulled out a couple of tubes of lip balm from her pocket. 'If you don't like the smell, you can put some of this inside. Would you prefer strawberry or chocolate?'

With some trepidation he pointed to the

chocolate-flavoured balm and Summer proceeded to spread some of it inside the mask.

'See?' She held the mask up for him to inhale the scent, giving him some say in what
was happening to him. Enough to convince
him to co-operate.

'I just have to go and put on some special
clothes so I can come to Theatre with you then
we'll be on our way.'

She'd had a word with Cody Brennan, one of
the clinic founders and the orthopaedic surgeon
who was performing the operation, and he'd
given the go-ahead for her to accompany Ben.

Although it was a relatively straightforward
procedure for Cody, who did this every day of
the week, it was a frightening experience for
a young child. She'd be on tenterhooks herself until the whole thing was over because
there were always risks associated with surgery. Not that she'd shown Ben any sign of her
own nerves.

'This is a relatively new procedure called
flexible intramedullary nailing but it's becoming popular to treat paediatric femur fractures,'
Cody explained to her.

'Sounds…complicated.' There wasn't any gentle way of joining bits of broken bone back together and she'd heard of metal plates, rods, pins and screws being involved so she supposed nails were simply another piece of hardware incorporated in the mechanics.

Californian Cody could be a bit stiff at times, unapproachable if you were easily intimidated, but she'd persuaded him to share the process to educate her in what went on behind the scenes.

'It does the job. We insert flexible nails through the end of the femur and across the injury site. This holds the bones in place while they heal.'

'How long will that take?' Maple Island Clinic was renowned for its modern approach to rehabilitation and breakthrough techniques and Cody specialised in lower-limb surgery so she was aware there must be a specific reason they'd be adopting this new technique.

'It will take about four months to completely heal then we'll remove the nails. The advantage is that there should be no limb-length inequality or visible scars that can result from other procedures and the leg won't require a cast.'

'So he'll be as good as new?'

'All being well, yes, he'll make a full recovery and bounce back to normal.'

She shut up then and let the surgeon do his thing, observing in awe. One of the things she loved about her job was getting to work so closely with children and following their progress through injury and illness, though there was always a danger of becoming too close to some of her patients.

Perhaps if she'd had a family of her own around her it wouldn't leave such a void in her life when her patients moved on, as they inevitably did. That didn't mean she should involve herself with a ready-made father and child. The problem with getting entangled with someone else's family was that one day another woman might come to claim them back.

An image of Gracie and Rafael sprang to mind but she tried to blank it out. The operation was a good diversion for her and the empty house waiting for her at the end of the night.

* * *

Once Ben was safely through his operation, Summer was ready to fall unconscious into bed, although she knew her brain was bound to spend countless hours replaying the time she and Rafael had had together, preventing sleep from coming too easily. Even if she ignored the tension they'd shared in the corridor, there were still so many feel-good moments to choose from today. From the feel of his muscles under his shirt to that electric contact between their fingertips, she could spend all night reading more into those brief touches than had probably been there.

She left the recovery ward and rounded the corner to let the ER staff know she was leaving, only to be confronted by Rafael and a weeping Graciela sitting in the corridor.

The initial shock of seeing him here and the urge to go back the way she'd come in case he guessed she'd been thinking about him was quickly countered by the sight and sounds of his daughter's distress.

'Oh, Gracie. What's happened?' She dropped

into the seat next to Rafael and leaned over to inspect the badly swollen ankle on view.

The exotic scent of his citrus and spice cologne teased her senses, so moreish it was making her hungry.

'Accident in the workplace,' he said with a grimace.

Summer surveyed the sight of Gracie's princess dress and her bent fairy wings and gave it her best guess. 'Trouble in Fairy Land?'

Was that a laugh she heard? The sound was so unexpected and devastating to her equilibrium she couldn't decide whether to crack another funny or render him mute for ever.

'I was picking up some files from my room and…er…we got a bit carried away spinning on the office chair.' Given how protective he was over his daughter, Summer could only imagine how much he was beating himself up over whatever had happened.

'Ouch. Poor baby,' she said, straightening Gracie's wings. Then she addressed Rafael. 'Has she been checked over yet?'

He leaned over to whisper to her, probably so Gracie couldn't hear, his black hair tickling the side of her face and conspiring to drive her senses crazy. 'I don't think she's broken anything but we can't get her to go in for an X-ray to be certain.'

It could be a scary place with all that machinery whirring in there. Gracie was already upset and under the fluorescent glare of the clinic lighting it was easy for her to become disoriented and confused. They needed to persuade her somehow so they could get a clear idea of what was going on with that foot and treat it accordingly, instead of leaving it to potentially worsen.

'I don't suppose… I mean I know we're not in day-care and it's not strictly your problem but you were able to work your magic with her this morning… Would you mind helping me get her in there?'

She knew it was taking everything in him to ask her as he fumbled to find the words. This was a huge step forward in her progress with him, which in turn might filter through to Gracie in accepting help. It wasn't obvious what had caused this turn-around and it could have been through sheer exhaustion rather than an acceptance that this was her area of expertise, but she wasn't going to question it.

'Give me a second.' An idea popped into her head about how they might be able to convince Gracie to co-operate and left them to go in search of the box of toys they'd have somewhere here to occupy the children in the waiting room.

A rummage around soon unearthed a raggedy-looking doll, a magnetic drawing board and a toy camera. Rudimentary perhaps but she often used toys to explain procedures to the children who perhaps required scans or X-rays, and it helped dispel some of that fear surrounding the unknown. She located a bandage, which she intended to tie around the doll's leg in exactly the same place as where Gracie had her injury, and she rushed back to the reluctant patient.

Rafael raised an eyebrow as he spotted the armful of toys she was carrying but for once he didn't question her plans or whisk Gracie away before she could implement them.

With him subdued, Summer seized her

chance to present her finds and offer her assistance.

'This is Dolly. She's had a bit of an accident and she's hurt her leg.' Summer set the doll on Rafael's knee so Gracie could see her from her vantage point on her father's shoulder.

Curious, she peered down to see what was going on. A good sign that she was engaged in proceedings.

'She was spinning around in the garden and fell over. She bumped her head and I guess she hurt her leg too.'

Her face full of concern, Gracie shuffled down Rafael's torso to sit on his other knee. 'Will she get better?'

To hear a full sentence, have her attention so fully, was a feat not often mastered and a great achievement on both sides. Although Summer didn't want to make a big fuss about it and send her back into that world lost to everyone but Gracie, it took a moment before she could speak herself. Rafael's Adam's apple bobbing up and down as he gulped didn't escape her notice either.

'The doctor can fix her if she'll let him take

an X-ray of her poorly leg. Do you know how to do that, Gracie?'

She shook her head.

'If I tell you how to do it then maybe you could be the doctor and help her?' Patient participation often helped the children understand what was going on and when she could she tried to make it as fun as possible for them.

Gracie looked to her father for guidance.

'You can do it, Dr Valdez.' Then he whispered in her ear, 'I think Dolly is a little frightened. She might need you to tell her it's going to be okay.'

Taking her new responsibilities very seriously, Gracie bent down to talk to her patient. 'Don't be scared. I'll make you better.'

'We have to lay her down to take a special photograph.' Summer's voice cracked with emotion at the focus Gracie was showing as she stretched the doll flat out on her father's knee.

'This is a special camera that will show the doctor where her leg hurts but she has to stay very still.' She handed over the camera and let

Gracie push the button while she sketched a crude picture of a leg bone on the board.

'Could we get your opinion on the X-ray, Dr Valdez Senior?' Summer held up her artistic rendering for Rafael's scrutiny while they both tried not to laugh at it.

His eyes were twinkling with emotion and suppressed laughter, his scowl finally fading, and her pulse raced in response. She liked this softer side of him, it made him even more attractive and she didn't see it nearly enough. He always looked so deadly serious she often longed to be the one to help him smile again, and now she had she might start acting the clown around him more often to make it a permanent fixture.

'Well…it's not broken. A bad sprain, I would say. We'll bandage it up and prescribe plenty of rest.'

'Dr Gracie?'

The younger doctor proceeded to wrap the bandage around Dolly's leg and Summer fastened it so it wouldn't come loose.

'She'll be as good as new in no time. Now, we have to fix you too, Gracie. Do you think the doctor could take a special photograph of your leg?'

She thought about it for a moment. 'Can you and Dolly come as well?'

'We might have to go into the room where the lady takes the photograph but Daddy can go in with you if he wears a special apron. He can hold your hand and we'll wave to you through the window.' Summer was sure they could talk the radiographer into a couple of extra guests for a few minutes.

'Gracie?' Rafael coaxed her some more until she finally nodded her consent and they quickly whisked her off to the X-ray department in case she changed her mind again.

'Thank goodness it was nothing more than a sprain. That's bad enough but I'd never have forgiven myself if she'd broken something.' Rafael had thought as much but the confirmation was a hundred times preferable to sheer hope. Apart from the guilt that had lain heavily on his conscience, an immobile Graciela would have driven them both insane. The injury would temporarily slow her down but a cumbersome cast would have been much worse for a lot longer.

'Rafael, accidents are part of childhood. Are you telling me you've never broken a bone or had stitches through misadventure?' Summer's blue eyes glittered with something he couldn't quite put his finger on. He couldn't tell if she was teasing him or referencing something in her own background. Whatever it was, he knew she was only doing it to make him feel better when he'd been such an absolute horror to her earlier today.

He couldn't find fault with anything she'd said or done since coming across them in the corridor. Quite the opposite. She'd done everything in her power to help them through this without judgement, criticism or a clear desire to get on with her own personal life. She'd had nothing to gain from staying on here with them and she'd gone out of her way to persuade Gracie into having that X-ray. He was glad to have had her with them.

The doll idea had been genius. Gracie still had it now, clutched in her hand as she slept on Summer's shoulder. Rafael wasn't going to attempt to take it off her and if it came to it he didn't think the staff would mind if he replaced Dolly with a new one from the store. Small things such as a black-haired doll who looked a bit like her could make life a little less stressful for a while.

Summer was still watching and waiting for an answer so he had to switch his thoughts from the present to a time he didn't often wish to visit. Except her gentle teasing on this occasion did evoke a memory he'd forgotten and made him groan.

He ran his finger over the small bump on the bridge of his nose. 'Broken nose at fifteen when I came off a motorbike.'

Summer cocked her head to one side as though trying to picture the scene. 'No offence but I didn't have you down as the grungy biker type.'

'I wasn't that impressive. It was my first time on a bike and I slid halfway across the road on my backside.'

'Were you wearing leathers? I mean, to protect you, not because I'm trying to imagine you in black leathers or anything…' As she rambled on, apparently fascinated by his apparel at the time, the honeyed tone of her skin took on a scarlet hue. It was the first time he could remember ever seeing her rattled and he did get a kick out of her losing her cool for a second. He couldn't help himself from teasing a little more to glimpse further into this girlish persona beyond Summer's usual professional façade.

'Um… I think I had the pants at least.' He caught her eye, his smile broadening as hers narrowed.

'It's good to know you, uh, had some protection,' she said, cringing with every ill-chosen word.

'Some, but I'm afraid it didn't save my dignity and it definitely didn't succeed in pulling off the rebellious act I'd been attempting.' The local teenagers had seemed so popular and carefree compared to him, and though he'd longed to be part of that crowd, his first foray into normality had failed spectacularly.

'What were you rebelling against?' He'd stirred Summer's interest in his life before Maple Island and that was something he didn't want anyone poking their noses into. This was his new start and he didn't wish to be reminded of the past and those in it. It hurt too much. Especially now he had a child of his own and couldn't imagine turning his back on her the way his parents had done to him. He loved his daughter unconditionally and only ever wanted the best for her, not himself.

'The usual teenage angst—parents, school, peers—and feeling generally hard done by. What about you? Something tells me you have a story or two to tell.' His upbringing might not have been as conventional as most but he figured he'd encountered the same emotional turmoil as anyone else, only on a different level. Summer, on the other hand, was such a force of nature and so unafraid of taking chances he could imagine trouble following her everywhere she went.

She gave him the side-eye and he knew he'd hit pay dirt. 'I may have broken my collarbone playing soccer in the UK, fractured my wrist punching a handsy drunk in Rome and, oh, I cracked a rib tombstoning from the cliffs into the sea in Turkey. Just the usual gap-year stuff.'

Hearing snippets of her previous life before coming to the island only made her more appealing to Rafael, even though it should give him more reason to avoid her. Anyone who'd braved such adventures would eventually get bored with island life when it could be so limiting. He'd chosen to come here for that stability, secure in the knowledge nothing would really change, but there wasn't much thrill-seeking to be had around here unless you counted being tempted by a co-worker.

'You've done a bit of travelling, then?' None of it surprised him and not only was he impressed, he was kind of jealous of her conviction to her fearless spirit. He'd had many dreams over the years but the only one he'd seen through had been his desire to go to medical school in America, and that had cost him his family.

'A bit. When my mom remarried I went a bit wild but I've got that bug out of my system. I'm happy where I am now.' It suggested she hadn't always been content with her lot but she'd fought for more. That part of him he was trying to keep at bay hoped she really did intend to stick around for good.

He'd witnessed her fierce spirit for himself today and it had made him think that if she'd had a daughter like his, if Gracie had had a mother like Summer, she would've fought for her with every fibre of her being, instead of abandoning her at the first sign of trouble.

Tonight was a prime example. Here she was, long past the end of her shift, carrying his daughter through the clinic because she refused to let go. That was an endorsement of her character when Gracie very rarely showed any signs of affection to anyone and even less to complete strangers. Clearly Summer had worked hard to earn her trust and he was witnessing the benefits of her experience and expertise first-hand.

If he'd paid more attention to the relationship she'd developed with his daughter instead of pushing her away to protect himself, he might've saved them all from this upset in the emergency room. Summer would've minded Gracie, no problem, for the short time it should've taken him to collect his things from the office.

As they stepped outside the warmth of the hospital, the night air took his breath away, along with the realisation he had potentially harmed his daughter by rebuffing Summer's earlier proposal.

She carried the sleeping bundle over to the car for him and attempted to deposit her into her seat but Gracie refused to let go. They were all exhausted and rather than face another tantrum, Rafael suggested he take Summer home en route. It was the least he could do considering everything she'd done for them tonight.

'Thanks.'

Rafael closed the rear door and left Summer to belt them both into the back seat. He paused, watching her fuss around Gracie, not thrilled with the knowledge he made her feel uncomfortable around him. It wasn't fair to jeopardise her bond with Gracie when she was helping her to make such great progress. Hearing her chat away like any other three-year-old tonight and seeing her playing with the toys had brought a lump to his throat and a swelling in his chest that she'd made it this far despite her challenges.

'So, um, where should I drop you off?' he asked in the rear-view mirror as he started the engine. Not knowing which part of the island she lived on suddenly seemed ignorant on his behalf when she was privy to so much about his own personal circumstances.

'Don't worry about me, I can walk from your place to mine. It's not too far and I'd rather you get Gracie to bed. She's had a long day.' She was yawning herself and Rafael had to stifle his own. At least they didn't have miles to drive. The whole island could be circumnavigated in a lunch hour. That also meant the inhabitants practically lived on top of one another, though some might be completely oblivious to anyone else outside their own front door.

'You live near us? I didn't realise.' He met her eyes in the mirror and wondered how that had escaped him. The beach house where he and Gracie resided was more secluded than some of the properties nearer town and he thought of Summer as someone who'd prefer to be close to the action rather than existing on the outskirts.

She broke eye contact and looked away. 'A little further down the beach, I think. I've seen you running down there.'

That would explain why he'd never noticed her out there. When he was running he blocked out everything around him, using that precious alone time to work through whatever problems were uppermost in his thoughts at that particular time. It wasn't easy to indulge his sporty side, stealing breaks in between appointments or taking advantage of having child-care for a few extra minutes in order to do so. As well as providing him with time out, it was important he keep his fitness levels up for his busy lifestyle and to ensure he'd be around as long as Gracie needed him.

A familiar sense of calm descended on him as they reached home and the comforting sound of the waves breaking nearby soothed his stretched nerves. By the time he got out and opened the front door Summer was already there with Gracie in her arms.

'I can put her to bed for you so we don't wake her. It's no problem.'

Rafael was thrown by the innocuous offer simply because of the implications of letting her inside. He didn't have people over. This was his and Gracie's safe space where they didn't have to worry about anyone judging them. They shut themselves away here night after night, locking the outside world away to leave them in their happy bubble inside. He was the one person he could rely on to keep Gracie safe, having been let down by those he'd trusted. If it happened again, if Gracie was put in jeopardy because he'd shared his parental responsibility with someone else, it would be his fault for leaving them in that position again.

Yet if tonight had taught him anything it was to stop being so defensive about the idea of someone helping and to start being kinder to Summer, who had done absolutely nothing except be her usual wonderful self.

It was past experiences keeping him from trusting her, not his current instincts. If he didn't have the painful memories of betrayal lodging with him and went with his gut on this, he knew he should be throwing the door wide open for her. She wasn't on the clock, this wasn't a cash inducement, and she'd have been well within her rights to leave him to struggle in that hospital corridor with Gracie. He had to accept she had his daughter's best interests at heart and they were both on the same side.

Perhaps it wasn't only his insecurities turning this simple act into a life-changing decision. For him, he knew letting Summer into his house was a decision to let her into his life on a personal level too. Once she stepped inside he was allowing her access to parts of his life he'd cordoned off since Christina had betrayed him in the worst possible way. It had seemed the only way to keep him and Gracie safe. By crossing the threshold tonight Summer would become the first woman to enter their home who was anyone other than a paid childminder.

As his silence stretched to the point of becoming awkward for both of them, he eventually had to grant her admission. He couldn't live in the past for ever, and Summer was showing him he had to start trusting people, if only to benefit Gracie.

'First door on the left at the top of the stairs.' He led the way, opening the child safety gates at the top and bottom of the steps, unsettled himself by the disruption of their bedroom routine. It would be churlish to insist on carrying Gracie himself when transferring her would simply increase the odds of waking her.

'We'll have to get these things off our Fairy Princess,' Summer whispered, as she sat down on the mattress with Gracie on her lap.

Rafael took a seat next to her on the small bed and began to slip Gracie's arms out of her coat. The sound of his heart was thumping in his ears at the proximity of Summer next to him.

'Sorry,' he mumbled, fumbling to remove the fairy wings without bumping against her and failing. His hand brushed against the softness of Summer's body and he daren't look to see which part of her he'd connected with in case he combusted through sheer awkwardness. He wasn't used to being so close to a woman in his home and certainly not in such a confined space. It was almost as if he'd forgotten how to act normally, so aware was he of her presence beside him.

'It's okay. I can get it from here.' Her voice was a little breathy too as they struggled to undress the unconscious three-year-old merely millimetres apart. She managed to unhook the wing closest to her but as she stretched to slip the other down Gracie's arm, her fingers grazed along his thigh. Every muscle in him tensed and every hair on his body stood to attention in anticipation of her making contact with him again.

She didn't apologise but they exchanged nervous smiles and he knew she was as aware of touching him as he was. This electric tension between them was a strange sensation for a man whose job it was to physically examine people every day of the week. It was as though they were afraid to touch each other because of some unforeseen consequence that would make this about more than simply putting his daughter to bed.

He hadn't considered the possibility Summer might be attracted to him the way he was to her but it was there in the coy look she gave him and the spot where she'd brushed against him. It was a reflection of his own desire and recognition that there was something happening between them far beyond their control. That took them into even more dangerous territory than he'd imagined. This validated whatever feelings he'd been having towards her and somehow made it all real, more acceptable.

He broke out of the vacuum they'd created between their bodies, where logic and common sense had been forced out, so they could manoeuvre Gracie under the covers. Once he'd pulled back the comforter, Summer laid her down with the same tenderness he would've done. They both tucked her in and watched her sleep like two proud parents and that's when he knew they had to leave. It was one thing to bond over his daughter but they shouldn't get carried away that it meant anything.

He turned out the light and tiptoed from the room, leaving Summer to ease the door shut behind them.

'Hopefully tonight's excitement will help

her sleep to a reasonable hour.' He kept his voice low so he wouldn't disturb her but he also found himself reluctant to move from the hallway. It seemed such an intimate act, putting his daughter to bed with her, and he was enjoying the closeness of sharing the moment after doing it alone for so long.

Summer rested her head against the door and smiled up at him. 'I don't know how you manage. I'm exhausted.' She covered her yawn with her hand.

'Through sheer determination and the help of clinic staff. I'm not sure we'd ever have made it home without you.'

'Nonsense. You're an amazing father. She's very lucky to have you.' The compliment wasn't having nearly as much effect on him as the way she was looking at him, eyes full of admiration and making him feel ten feet tall.

They stood in silence, Rafael being drawn closer and closer into her personal space and leaving no room for fear about where this could lead.

Summer tilted her mouth up towards him, so soft and tempting and proving beyond doubt that none of these strange new feelings were one-sided.

Yet in that second he knew the next move would decide if she was to be in their lives for his or his daughter's needs. There was no competition.

He swallowed back any lustful thoughts and focused on everything she could offer Gracie.

'Summer, I… I'd like to take you up on your offer to look after Gracie permanently. We'll have to okay it with the clinic directors but I think it would be for the best after all.'

CHAPTER FOUR

SUMMER BLINKED, HOPING it would somehow bring things back into focus for her. For a minute she'd thought Rafael had been about to kiss her and she'd wanted him to. She'd had to put her fingers to her lips to make sure she wasn't still puckered up, waiting for it.

She knew she had been fantasising about him a lot recently but it couldn't have been all in her imagination because she certainly wouldn't have moved in for a kiss unless he'd leaned in first. He'd obviously had second thoughts in the nick of time, deeming his devotion to his daughter's welfare a higher priority than a spur-of-the-moment kiss. The lapse in judgement had most likely come from tiredness and gratitude and nothing personal that would warrant her jeopardising her position at the clinic anyway. An admirable move that she would appreciate more once she scuttled back out of his home to hide her embarrassment under cover of darkness.

She'd clearly done her job well enough tonight to convince him she could take care of his daughter. If they had kissed, their working relationship would've become untenable and she doubted the clinic management would've looked favourably upon her if they thought she made a habit of coming on to the dads at daycare.

'Sure. That would be great,' she said, much too brightly for someone whose ego was gradually shrivelling up the further Rafael backed away from her. 'I'll speak to the bosses tomorrow and we can work out a schedule as best we can.' One that entailed their only interaction from now on would be solely based around the handover of Gracie's care.

'Will you be okay walking home?' His polite, if unsubtle, query was his way of telling her he wanted her to get the hell out of his house.

'I'll be fine. I'll enjoy the walk.' She practically stumbled down the stairs in her haste to get away from him and the situation she'd found herself in.

He didn't even try to follow her and simply called out, 'I'll see you tomorrow.'

Summer let herself out onto the porch and the cold air seemed to sizzle against her red-hot skin. At least the non-kiss meant she could face him at work with a fraction of her dignity still intact. If they'd actually locked lips *then* thought about the consequences and pretended the moment hadn't happened, the rejection would've stung even more than it did now.

She pulled her coat around her to keep the chill from penetrating the rest of her body and stepped down onto the sand. It was dark but the sky was clear, the moon providing enough light for her to see where she was going. This was her peaceful place. The waves breaking on the shore always managed to calm the tangle of the thoughts in her head when she'd had a rough day and this one had been a doozy.

The Boston lights on the horizon reminded her of the life and the people she'd left behind. Whilst she regretted the circumstances that had brought her out here, it was the best move she'd ever made and she didn't intend to make the same mistake twice. There was no way she was giving up a job she loved and moving because she'd got involved with the wrong man again. She was the one who'd end up alone and in pain.

'Are you sure you can't have the chef rustle up some eggs Benedict for me? I'm sure he's heard of it. That is if he didn't get his qualifications off the back of a cereal box.' Philomena Kerridge-Bates could be heard all over the rehab unit as Rafael walked through the main recovery ward on his way to the children's ward and witnessed her pushing away her breakfast.

'You don't want all that fancy nonsense. What you need is a bowl of good old oatmeal, thick enough to stand on. That'll soon build you up,' Old Salty yelled across at her, dispensing his prescription for her recovery.

'It sounds revolting. I thought this was supposed to be a first-class establishment? Why am I being subjected to this treatment?' She fanned her face with the bone-handled fan she'd apparently brought with her to deal with the shock of such eventualities. The harassed girl who'd brought the offending food offering scuttled off, no doubt to have a breakdown in the kitchen along with the other staff attempting to cater to her needs. She was a paying client so there wasn't much could be done about her attitude to the staff or the facilities except to try and pacify her. However, Old Salty was under no obligation to be polite and apparently regularly put her in her place.

'You have a bed, three hot meals a day and people at your beck and call. What more do you need, woman?' Her portly foe spoke with his mouth full of toast before slurping it down with his orange juice. The wink he gave Rafael made him think he was doing this on purpose to get under her skin but as long as they had each other to duel with, Rafael was keeping out of it.

'Some manners would be good, Mr Harrington,' Mrs Kerridge-Bates sniffed as she laid a linen napkin across her lap. Rafael had an inkling Salty would be making a point of ensuring she wasn't going to get everything her own way while he was around.

Rafael carried on to the children's beds to check up on his youngest patients, Peyton and Connor Walsh, who'd suffered severe spinal trauma after an accident with some scaffolding. He'd operated on them in Boston, removing shards of wood from Peyton's thoracic spine and performing the new mini-scaffolding procedure on Connor. The three-dimensional bandage should heal his cracked vertebrae and Alex Kirkland, who specialised in the leg and walking lab, was working towards helping the children walk again.

That pioneering operation had attracted the clinic's attention and he had these two to thank for bringing him and Graciela to Maple Island so he had a special attachment to the case.

'Morning.' He hadn't expected to find Summer in here with them.

'Morning.' Summer was clearly not as excited about seeing him as the Walsh children were, who greeted him with a simultaneous, 'Hi!'

Thank goodness they'd seen sense last night

and avoided that kiss or things could've become awkward. It was more important his daughter have stability and understanding with someone she trusted than giving in to a spur-of-the-moment temptation. It had felt like the most natural thing in the world to lean in for a kiss after tucking Gracie into bed for the night. The chemistry had certainly been there between them and she'd suddenly become part of their little bubble, isolated from the rest of the world outside. In his home, far from real life at the clinic, he hadn't been thinking about responsibility or the repercussions of what they had been doing. Only that he'd wanted to kiss her.

The irony had been when she'd made it clear the feeling was mutual, giving him pause for thought. He knew giving in to temptation would affect them both and so he had pulled them back from the brink of a mistake just in time. Since she'd agreed to his proposal about reconsidering Gracie's care on a more regular basis, they'd have to get over their personal issues pretty quickly. There was no room for embarrassment or attraction lest it impact on his daughter in any way.

'What have we got here?' The children were both sitting up in their adjacent beds with Summer between them, surrounded by art supplies and smiles. She split her time between the day-care centre and her patients here when she could to check on the twins' welfare, so it wasn't unusual to find her in residence. It was simply the timing which had thrown him.

'I thought we could try some art therapy today to see how Peyton and Connor are feeling about their time here and their progress.' Summer was perfectly civil as she addressed his curiosity but she couldn't quite meet his eye. Something he was going to have to work on if she was ever to trust he wouldn't make another advance towards her.

He peeked at the two canvases the twins were painting to get an idea of how they were feeling about their long road to recovery.

'May I?' He checked with them before taking a closer look in case these were private expressions not intended for anyone else to see, merely an outlet for frustrations they hadn't been able to communicate thus far.

There was no such hesitation in showing off their masterpieces so all credit went to their teacher for encouraging their efforts.

'Mine first.' Connor, the more confident of the two, held his up and waved it as if it was a winning lottery ticket.

Careful not to get any wet paint on his hands or his clean shirt before he did the rest of his rounds, Rafael took the canvas. The word 'WINNER!' was crudely written in thick black letters surrounded by an explosion of colourful splodges he thought might be ticker tape.

'I beat Peyton yesterday in rehab,' he explained with glee as his competitor stuck out her tongue.

'That's great. You're both doing so well.' Whilst some healthy competition focused in the right direction could aid a faster recovery, he didn't want Peyton to become self-conscious that she wasn't progressing as well as her brother.

'Yes, but my injuries were worse than yours. Weren't they, Doctor?' Peyton showed she was equally as feisty and there was no way she was going to be left behind.

'I'm a miracle of science.'

They competed to be crowned champion of the spinal unit but they were both winners in his eyes and he would never pick one over the other.

'Let's see what you've got, Peyton.' He deflected the beginning of an argument to see what she'd painted, praying they wouldn't force him to pick which one he preferred.

Although the colours—soft pinks and baby blues—weren't as in your face as Connor's, the word in the centre of the painting didn't have any less impact.

'Brave'.

They couldn't have described themselves any more accurately with a four-thousand-word essay. Especially when there were so many negative emotions they could've exhibited given their circumstances. It said a lot about their strength of character and the amazing staff surrounding them. Summer included.

'I didn't realise we had such talented artists in our midst, did you, Miss Ryan?' To maintain some sort of professional distance he'd decided to address her more formally and remind himself that due to her role in his life they should no longer be on familiar terms.

He was impressed today, not only with the twins' resilience but by the methods she'd used to gauge their states of mind. It was easy to forget how important her role was here as a child life specialist as well as in the nursery when she downplayed it so well, but the psychological welfare of the patients was every bit as important as their physical recovery.

As the children's wing expanded they'd have more need for her in this capacity when she provided such a positive experience for the children in between their medical procedures. He knew that would take her away from Gracie but she'd be starting school eventually and hopefully Summer would continue to job-share until then.

'They've done really well. I'll have to find somewhere special to hang them.' She began to pack away the art supplies, no doubt due in her other role at the nursery now since he'd already dropped Gracie off there.

'I think you both deserve a treat,' Rafael bent down to whisper. 'What about something from the bakery?'

'Yay! You mean Brady's, right, and not that vegan one my mom likes?' Connor shuddered and Rafael put his mind at rest with a nod. 'In that case, I'll have a crème doughnut.'

'Can I have a chocolate sprinkle doughnut, please?' Peyton added her request too and her obvious excitement at such a small gesture made him wish these kids could get back to their normal lives as soon as possible.

'Shh. Keep the noise down or everyone will want one.' He'd check with their parents but he was sure they wouldn't object to them having a small treat.

'What about Summer?'

'Yeah. Doesn't she deserve a doughnut too?'

They petitioned on her behalf for a share in their success and he couldn't deny such a request.

'Sure. Perhaps Miss Ryan would come and tell me which sweet treat she'd prefer and we'll let Dr Alex get on with your rehab.' As fair-haired Alex approached the children's bedside it became clear Rafael and Summer were no longer required and neither would want to step on his toes when Alex was the one now leading their case.

'Yes, I'll have to get in quickly before there are none of my favourites left.' She was humouring him and the children but she did gather her supplies and follow him out into the corridor, leaving Alex to carry out his assessment.

'They both seem to be in good spirits, all things considered.' He debated whether or not to walk away and avoid a one-to-one with her but not only would that be immature, it wouldn't do much to improve their working relationship when they were about to become closer than ever thanks to Gracie.

Summer tucked the large sketch book under her arm. 'Yes. Obviously, our positive reinforcement is having an impact. At this stage I don't think they need extra counselling regarding their stay at the clinic.'

The twins would have needed therapy to overcome the trauma of the accident itself but often the long-term confinement to the hospital bed could be just as distressing.

'I think being here together has helped them settle in. I can see how Connor's competitiveness is spurring on Peyton's recovery.' That sibling rivalry would give them the determination to overcome their injuries, if only to get one up on each other.

'Yes, he's helpful in his unique way.' She smiled directly at him and Rafael took it as a sign she'd forgiven him and wanted to move past last night as much as he did.

'They've come a long way since I first treated them back in Boston, and as much as I love seeing them I'm looking forward to the day when they can walk out of here.'

'Me too. Well, I suppose I should get back to my other job before your daughter comes looking for me. How is she this morning?'

'Still a bit sore and having trouble putting weight on the ankle, which is making her more challenging than usual.' Gracie had been particularly fractious this morning, to the point of refusing to walk at all, so he'd had to carry her into nursery. He had hoped Summer would've been there to calm her down until he finished work and had more time to pander to her. They'd both been disappointed to find her not there.

Since this meeting had proved his urge to see her wasn't apparently to apologise for last night or have her hurry back to the nursery, he had to conclude he'd simply wanted an excuse to see her. Not everything had been solved by resisting that kiss. Preventing it happening didn't automatically stop him from thinking about what might have been.

'In that case, I should get over there and see if I can take her mind off it.'

'She won't put that doll down so I think you've got two patients to contend with.' The only way he'd got her to leave the house had been to promise Summer would help make Dolly feel better, and he wasn't fond of making promises he couldn't keep. Even if they were made on someone else's behalf.

'I think I can handle it,' she said with a laugh to ease his conscience.

'Good. Are we still on for your future career as a Gracie shadow too?' He tried to convince himself that was the real reason he'd sought her out, that he hadn't stuffed things up and could still count on her to do the right thing by Gracie.

'Of course. I'll have a chat with my manager when I get a chance.'

'I'll hang on here and have a word with Alex too. See if we can make it official.' As a father himself, it might be beneficial to get his boss's thoughts off the record about if he thought this was a good idea. He'd leave out the bit about almost kissing another member of staff, although since Alex had got together with Maggie Green, a physiotherapist here, he couldn't very well complain about workplace romance.

'No problem. Let me know if he's on board before we say anything to Gracie.' They stared at each other a heartbeat too long before she added, 'All right, then. 'Bye,' and walked away.

Rafael was still there to see her face light up when she stopped for a chat with Kaylee. She was a different person with her friend, laughing and carefree and a world away from a deadly serious single dad with more personal issues than she'd probably covered in her psychology training.

It was then he realised he had nothing to offer her even if he did like her on a personal level. He wouldn't want to curtail her fun but a relationship with a single parent carried a lot of baggage that was bound to weigh her down. It wouldn't be fair to clip her wings with the responsibilities of a family when she had so much more living to do before she settled down. He couldn't whisk her away on spontaneous romantic breaks or take her clubbing into the early hours of the morning the way a single man could. Before he did anything, he had to consider Gracie and that meant Summer would always have to come second. She deserved to be someone's number one and be spoiled with time and affection. The most he could give her was himself but even that came with stipulations. By entering into a relationship with him, Summer would be forced into a mothering role for Gracie that neither of them were probably ready for yet. It was best for Summer if they leave their one indiscretion in the past. She would get over it quicker than he would.

His chest hurt so badly at the thought of her moving on with another man he was sure that sadistic Cupid had taken a pot shot at him in a cruel prank.

CHAPTER FIVE

SUMMER PULLED A napkin from the dispenser and ripped it into tiny shreds, littering the table with tissue snowflakes. Fiona Brady, the co-owner with her husband, wouldn't be pleased she was making a mess in her spotless bakery and bistro or, worse, might come over to see what had her in such a flap, but she had to release some of this nervous energy somewhere. She daren't order a coffee before Kaylee got there or she'd be buzzing like a bug in a bottle on her second cup.

The waitress, one of the redheaded Brady offspring, was hovering but she hoped once her friend got here and they ordered, she'd give them some privacy. She needed to get some advice about this idea of working closer with Rafael, especially after what had almost happened last night. Since Kaylee had registered

Summer's personal interest before she had, she seemed the logical choice for a confidante.

It was obvious Rafael wanted to keep things strictly professional. He'd made that clear last night when he'd avoided that kiss and all but thrown her out of his house. Then had reinforced his stance by carrying on as though nothing had happened. Working in the same clinic, sometimes with the same patients, including his daughter, it was probably for the best.

The waitress passed by and gave a puzzled glance at the confetti she'd shed all over the table. Summer brushed it into her hand and shoved it in her pocket before she reported it back to her mother.

Her heart and her stomach flipped as a familiar figure crossed the road towards the café but it wasn't the person she'd been expecting.

'Hi, Rafael, Gracie.' There was no way of avoiding them when she'd chosen the seat closest to the door to give her an unobstructed view of Main Street.

'Hey.' He walked past her towards the counter, allowing her internal body parts to stop somersaulting. Gracie, however, pulled out a chair next to her and sat down with Dolly.

Her father put in the doughnut order the twins had requested and Gracie's sugar cookie. 'Er, Miss Ryan? Can I get you something? I did promise.'

'Summer,' Gracie shouted without looking up from Dolly, who was hopping across the table on her good leg with some assistance.

'Pardon?' Rafael was noticeably perplexed by her response.

'Not Miss Ryan, Papa. Summer.'

Summer suppressed a smirk that one of the Valdez family was showing some maturity to ensure they remained on first-name terms and his eye roll at the correction didn't escape her attention.

'Sorry, *Summer*, would you like something from the case?' Under pressure from his three-year-old, he was being overly nice now.

'No, thanks. I'm waiting for someone. I'll order when they get here.' She gave him a friendly smile and was surprised to see his features darken in response.

'Gracie, we should go and let Miss… Summer

get her coffee in peace.' He snatched up the cake box from the counter and held the door open to leave.

'Did you get to speak to Alex about that matter we discussed?' She knew he hadn't, because her supervisor at the day-care centre had still been completely in the dark when she'd raised the subject of Gracie.

'Not yet. I got a little…distracted.'

'Let me know if you've changed your mind about the arrangement, or when you want me to start.'

He grunted some unintelligible response as he urged Gracie out of the premises with him. Summer waved them out, wondering what on earth had happened to put him in such a foul mood.

'Sorry I'm late.' Kaylee rushed in through the door and Summer was forced to drag her attention away from the father and daughter crossing back over the road. It was none of her business what was bothering him.

'Hello.' Kaylee waved a hand in front of her face to remind her she was there.

'Sorry. Dr Valdez was just here. He seemed upset about something.'

'What is it with you two? You always seem to rub each other up the wrong way.' Summer's coffee companion dumped her purse on the table and collapsed into the chair opposite.

'That's not strictly true. We both care about what's best for Gracie, that's all. In fact, we've been discussing the idea of me caring for her on a full-time basis.'

'Do you really think that's a good idea?'

'Why?'

'I've seen the way you look at him.' The raised eyebrows were enough to make Summer blush.

'He's a good-looking guy but we're both professional. Nothing's going to happen.' Despite planning to confide in her friend about the near-kiss, she decided there was nothing to tell and should simply put the matter behind her the way Rafael had clearly done.

'Is that so? In that case, it might be a good idea for the two of you to take a step back rather than get closer where there's more temptation. Now, we should probably order before they throw us out.'

'I guess. I'll have an Americano, thanks.'

'And to eat?'

'You choose.' Summer had zero appetite, her stomach in knots that her wayward feelings for Rafael were apparently so transparent. Kaylee was right, she needed a buffer between her and the man she hadn't been able to stop thinking about since last night, and he needed more people in his life than her.

She reached for her bag and the notebook and pen she kept there to jot down some sort of schedule for her and Gracie that would keep her too busy to think about Rafael.

It was only then she saw Dolly lying under the table and knew she couldn't go home until she'd returned her to her rightful owner.

'And you just complicated matters even more,' she muttered to her soft-bodied friend. If Gracie was as attached to Dolly as Rafael had indicated, she'd have to return her tonight. Against her better judgement her pulse was racing at the prospect of seeing him again so soon.

* * *

'We'll get Dolly now, Gracie.' Rafael had tried to placate her with every other toy in the house rather than walk back into the café and look as though he was using his daughter as an excuse to spy on whoever Summer was meeting in the bakery.

In the end he decided her wrath was preferable to his daughter's, which experience had told him could last for hours. He'd heard enough screaming, crying and smashing things for one night and right now all he cared about was making her happy.

He parked the car across the street from Brady's, unbuckled Gracie from her car seat and prepared to interrupt Summer's coffee date. She'd looked so nervous and guilty when he'd spotted her in there he was convinced she had to be meeting up with another man.

Jealousy was something he hadn't experienced in a long time and he couldn't say he enjoyed the realisations it brought with it. She had moved on after their near-kiss. That's what he'd wanted. Except he hadn't expected it to happen so soon. Not when the memory was still so fresh for him he could still feel her breath on his lips. Despite all the reasons he shouldn't be with Summer, that's exactly where he wanted to be. Envy of the man who would have that privileged position twisted through his body like fast-acting poison, eating away at his insides and turning everything toxic.

Then he saw Summer walk out the door, talking to Dolly and, taking Gracie by the hand, he strode straight towards her.

'We were just coming to find you.'

'Me or my friend?' she asked, waving Dolly's arm at him, her adorable playfulness only furthering his pain.

'Gracie wouldn't go to bed without her.' That was the understatement of the century and couldn't begin to convey the chaos that had ensued as a result of Dolly's disappearance. He'd torn the house and car apart looking for her to calm Gracie down before realising she'd been left as a gooseberry on Summer's date.

'Now she doesn't have to.' Summer handed her over with a smile that he only ever wanted to be for him.

'Thanks. Did you…uh…have a nice time?'

He didn't know why he'd asked when the thought was physical and mental torture to him and the answer was written all over her face anyway.

Her frown disappeared as quickly as it had formed as she probably wondered why he thought it was any of her business who'd she'd been with, or what they'd done. 'I did, as it happens. Kaylee's good company.'

'Kaylee…yeah, she seems like fun.' Relief whooshed through him so quickly at the mention of her colleague at the nursery his head was spinning. The knowledge that she wasn't seeing another man after all revealed some home truths to Rafael. He'd convinced himself he couldn't be with her but the thought of her with someone else had eaten away at him at such a devastating rate it was clear this was more than simple attraction. There were feelings developing for her that went beyond superficial desires but understanding that didn't mean he was in any better a place to act on them.

'Actually, I was noting down a few ideas about some fundraising events we could do to pay for some more beds in the children's wing.' She rummaged in her bag and it was his turn to wonder why he should be involved.

'I'm sure it will be much appreciated. Let me know what I can do.' The clinic already funded a couple of beds for those families who couldn't afford their children's medical expenses and he knew an extension to the charitable cause could only be a good thing.

'I was hoping you would volunteer to organise it,' she said with a grimace as he prepared to end his involvement with a donation.

'Me? Why?' He was stopped in his tracks by the suggestion and couldn't figure out where this idea had come from.

'In case you haven't noticed, a lot of the events on Maple Island are based around food. I was thinking perhaps we could promote a healthier option by having a sponsored triathlon. I know it's still too cold to expect people to go swimming in the sea, so we might be able to do something at the clinic. It shouldn't be too hard to get control of the pool for the swimming event and set up some exercise bikes and treadmills for the cycling and running.'

'Sounds good but I don't understand where I come in.' She'd obviously put a lot of thought into the idea and, although admirable, he didn't understand why she would then want him to take over the reins and claim the glory.

'That's a funny story… You have a bit of a nickname around here—Triathlon Dad.' She was trying to conceal a smirk and failing.

'Okay,' he said, not really understanding the joke.

'On account of all the sport you do around the island,' she explained, and this time he got it. The swimming, cycling and running he did apparently hadn't gone unnoticed.

'I had no idea.' He shook his head with a laugh. It was kind of funny when he'd always imagined he'd managed to keep a low profile on the island outside the clinic.

Summer glanced at Gracie, who was too busy playing with Dolly to care what the grown-ups were talking about, and lowered her voice. 'Anyway, I thought it might do you good to integrate into the community more.'

He bristled at the thought of inviting more people into his life when he was still experiencing the fallout from bending his house rules for her. 'Gracie and I are quite happy as we are, thank you.'

'I just thought…well, have you ever considered that by closing yourself off you're also limiting Gracie's social skills even more?' She bit her lip, clearly knowing how close she was pushing his patience to the limit.

He didn't appreciate anyone telling him how to raise his daughter but Summer's opinion was one he was learning to respect. Everything she said made sense even if it sometimes felt like a slight against his parenting skills. Something he now knew she would never intentionally do.

It occurred to him that this exercise in public relations she was proposing might provide some distraction from his growing attraction to her. Their closeness could have been precipitated by his limited social circle since coming to Maple Island and he supposed it wouldn't hurt to extend it a little. If they had other things, other people to keep them busy, they might stop seeking each other out.

'I guess it's worth looking into and it's for

a good cause after all.' The clinic, and those who came to it, would benefit from the fund-raising. He glanced at Gracie as she clutched her second-hand doll and considered the possibility that in trying to protect her, he'd isolated her more. Something he wanted a chance to rectify for her sake.

'I'm not sure of your family circumstances, and do feel free to tell me to mind my own business, but do you have any family who might come over for the event? It might be a good excuse for them to come and visit, perhaps spend some time with Gracie.' She was fishing now, looking for someone else he could invite into his daughter's life, but that wasn't an option.

'No one local,' was all the information he was prepared to give.

He thought about his parents for the first time in years. When Christina had first left, when his life had been in utter chaos, he'd considered contacting his family. He'd needed to reach out to someone for that support most people took for granted in their lives, but by then Gracie's developmental issues had become apparent. With a future stretching ahead of them already full of uncertainty, he'd shut down any possibility of inviting his parents back into his personal business.

Someday he might forgive them for their lack of compassion towards him but he didn't want to leave Gracie susceptible to the same treatment. If they were to reject her for not fitting in to the mould of their perfect grand-child, he knew he would never forgive them. For now, he would rather leave things as they were so no one else got hurt.

Summer's apparent step too far into Rafael's personal affairs was disrupted by the sound of squealing brakes, followed by an almighty crash. They both paused, and the ensuing silence was as frightening as the initial din. It became clear someone close by might be hurt and requiring assistance. After rushing back round the corner, they saw a scene of devastation that was too close to home not to affect them.

The second she saw Rafael's silver sedan crushed between the two other vehicles she had to brace herself before her legs gave way. It had been shunted into the stationary car in front by the one currently wedged into the back of it. No one could have survived that double impact and she was grateful they'd been with her instead. The alternative didn't bear thinking about.

'It's okay, Gracie.' She comforted the little girl, who was understandably upset at the sight, and quickly moved to block the scene from Gracie's view.

A crowd had gathered around the station wagon slammed sideways into Rafael's car and once she'd convinced him she would look after Gracie, he sprinted across the road to help.

Every now and then he glanced up at her from his crouched position on the ground where he was talking to the injured driver, his face a conflicting mixture of emotions that weren't difficult to interpret. She knew him well enough to see he was thankful he and Gracie were safe but worried for everyone else involved. All of which he was setting aside to help the injured. Her heart swelled, full of admiration for the man he was, not only as a committed medical professional but also as a compassionate human being. So often she'd seen him put the needs of others first and not everyone she'd encountered in life was so noble.

He flashed her a brief smile, which was every bit as brief and unsteady as hers but proof enough to Summer he was glad she was there for him and Gracie.

The assembled crowd worked on prising the mangled car door open on the driver's side to enable access for the emergency services. With this level of trauma they had to be careful to stabilise the patient until she was transported and assessed to prevent any further damage being caused. Rafael was trying to calm the woman, who was rambling and crying about the brakes failing and, most worryingly, that she couldn't move her legs.

The ambulance pulled up alongside and the paramedics dispersed the crowd so they could reach the injured party. Rafael relayed the events and it was only when the woman had been given urgent pain relief and stabilised with a backboard and cervical collar that he was able to take a step back and breathe.

'I'll come with you back to the clinic,' he told the crew as he came back to check on Gracie. 'Thanks for helping, Summer.'

'I'm just glad you're both safe.' Drop-down-on-her-knees-weeping-and-wailing glad, though she couldn't show it in public.

'I can't believe how close we came.' He ran his hands over his head, his hair and confidence visibly ruffled for the first time since taking charge of the incident.

'You couldn't have known that was going to happen and you weren't hurt, that's the main thing.' She knew he'd never have forgiven himself if Gracie had been injured, no matter how faultless he'd have been in what happened.

'On initial assessment I think I'm going to be required at the clinic to treat the family before we can transfer them to Boston.'

'It didn't look good.' Maple Island didn't have a major trauma unit and they'd have to be flown to Boston, but not before they at least knew the extent of their injuries.

Rafael shook his head. 'It's going to be a long night.'

'I could take Gracie back to yours if you'd like? Will we have a sleepover, Gracie?' This wasn't in her plans for creating more distance between her and their family but she knew that right now Rafael wouldn't let anyone else help and neither would Gracie. She was alone in that privileged position and this was more about the patient getting the treatment she needed than her private life.

'With Dolly too?'

'With Dolly.' She was grateful if that was the child's only concern and hopefully she'd managed to keep her far enough away from everything going on to bother her.

Rafael scooped Gracie into his arms for an understandably too-long hug and Summer had to look away, choked up by the unsaid words and unexpressed emotions filling the air.

'I'll check in with you when I can,' he shouted, and jumped into the back of the ambulance.

As the ambulance raced to the clinic Rafael wished he had more time to process what had happened. In all likelihood, and despite not having all of the equipment readily available in the major trauma unit of a city hospital, he was going to have to operate on the driver of the car, if only to stabilise her until they could transfer her to Boston. As always, he'd leave his personal problems outside the doors of the operating room but for now his mind was a whirl of emotions that were going to take a while to work through.

His first thoughts always belonged to Graciela and how he could've lost her if she'd been strapped into the back seat when the car had slammed into his.

That picture of twisted metal and shattered glass, the vehicle crumpled beyond recognition, would haunt him for ever. His shudder was a reaction to the thought of the injuries she could've sustained and how empty his life would be without her in it.

Summer had reassured him immediately in the aftermath. 'She's fine.'

Hearing her say it had released the pressure in his lungs so he'd been able to inhale a shaky breath. She'd interpreted his actions so easily he knew she'd felt as concerned as he had.

The emergency room was a hive of activity as staff buzzed around the new patients, the drama of which he was sure hadn't been seen here before at the clinic. It was more akin to the high-paced environment of its city counterparts. Thankfully he was used to working in this kind of situation and entered with determination to bring some focus to it. Although he was aware this wasn't his department and the staff were more than capable, he wanted to be there in case he was needed.

Rafael presented himself to the lead physician overseeing the initial assessment and shook his hand.

'Am I glad to see you here. I've ordered X-rays but most of the pain appears to be centred around her spine.'

There were a lot of serious problems associated with high-impact accidents such as head, neck, chest or abdomen injuries and fractures. All of those would be referred to the relevant specialists but a further spinal injury could be prevented from causing more pain or deformity by initial surgery, and that was his area of expertise. Rafael wasn't in the habit of boasting but he knew there wasn't a better spinal surgeon to be found in Boston because he was here on Maple Island, and one of the first on the scene with first-hand knowledge of the traumatic event.

While waiting for the X-ray results, Rafael sought permission to do his own clinical evaluation on their adult patient. There was absolutely no hesitation from the attending physician in granting him access in the desire to expedite her treatment.

He applied progressive circular pressure to pinpoint where she was experiencing the tenderness but Paisley, the patient, was letting him know that everything he did hurt.

Potential injuries caused by the crash could include vertebrae fractures, disc extrusion, compression or carotid arterial injury. A cervical injury was often indicated by neurological discrepancy or obvious fracture or malalignment but it was too risky to perform a full range of motion assessment, given the high-impact collision she'd suffered and that she was experiencing neck pain, spine tenderness and was unable to even sit up.

She'd required a series of X-rays where all seven vertebrae had been visible and he'd consult Alex on this one too for a neurological exam measuring sensation, muscle tone and reflexes.

He was going to have to potentially stabilise the spine, remove bone fragments and restore the alignment of the vertebrae to reduce compression in the spinal cord.

If the vertebrae in the spinal cord were unsuitable he might have to perform a spinal fusion with metal plates, screws wires and metal rods. In some cases it was even possible to use small pieces of bone from the hip or knee to grow and fuse vertebrae, but he wouldn't know until he saw the damage for himself.

Rafael was more aware than ever that his patient's quality of life had literally been in his hands. The trauma she'd sustained to her spine would take a long period of healing and he'd wanted to give her every chance of getting back to normal. If they'd transferred her to

Boston immediately there'd have been a risk of causing more damage.

The excessive displacement of the spine had required a spinal fusion to stabilise the vertebrae. It had taken over three hours, using metalwork and bone grafts, to do the job so the body would eventually build bony bridges across those segments to prevent movement and the resulting pain.

As Paisley was wheeled into Recovery, with the drainage tubes protruding from her wound, the drip attached to replace lost fluids, and an oxygen mask to ease her breathing, he pictured himself in her place. A lapse in concentration and split-second decisions were all that had saved him from a similar fate.

What would've happened to Gracie in those circumstances? Paisley was going to be incapacitated for quite a while and there was all the follow-up treatment after that—physiotherapy to improve mobility, occupational therapy to manage daily activities once taken for granted, and a psychologist to work through the mental trauma she'd suffered throughout. In the same position, he was afraid he'd have to put Gracie into care.

Fortunately, the patient had family and friends in Boston able to step up and provide support for her. He had no one. His family had made the decision to cut him out of their lives when he'd chosen to live the life he wanted and buck tradition. However, when it came to friends he was entirely responsible for his own resistance to let anyone close enough to claim that title.

Now, imagining himself on that hospital trolley, perhaps with his daughter lying injured on another, he knew Summer was the only person he'd want by his side.

Here she was tonight, once again going beyond her duty to devote time to his daughter. She wasn't the sort of person who'd abandon Gracie without a second thought, the way her mother had. It was time he admitted the truth. That he was afraid another person he cared for would walk out on him again, leaving him to pick up the pieces of his broken heart and start over again. After being abandoned by his parents and Christina, he knew he wouldn't survive another.

When he'd first arrived in America, it had been a lonely experience as well as a cultural shock. Although fluent in several languages, including English, he'd had difficulty fitting into college life, unused to sharing his space with people who weren't family. It had taken time for him to acquire a small group of friends to socialise with, to confide in and generally spend time with. Up until then he'd had to wander the campus on his own, figuring out things for himself. Unlike other freshman students, he hadn't had the comfort of a familiar voice on the end of the telephone to reassure him things would work out. He'd been homesick without having a home to return to if things hadn't worked out.

Christina had been one of those who'd helped him fit in, always there to buck him up when he'd needed it, and falling for her had been inevitable when they'd spent so much time together. When she'd left he'd been taken right back to those early days, feeling abandoned and totally alone in the world. Except this time he'd had a helpless baby to take care of too. Since then it had been him and Gracie against the world and it was only recently he'd stopped thinking of himself as being alone.

Summer had shown affection for them both and had made a difference in his life and Gracie's. To lose her in any capacity would create a hole in his life that could never be filled. Not when he could sense the chance of happiness almost within his grasp.

Summer represented a danger to his status quo but that safety net he'd strung up around him and Gracie now felt more restrictive and suffocating than sharing his space with someone who cared for them.

He was exhausted from taking care of Gracie and working but they loved life on the island and he didn't want anything to spoil that. He'd thought he was protecting his heart by envisioning the worst-case scenario if he entered into another relationship. Now he was wondering if he wasn't doing them all a disservice by maintaining this detachment from the rest of the world.

CHAPTER SIX

RAFAEL LET HIMSELF into the house to find a sleeping Summer curled up on the couch. Seeing her waiting for him after the long, stressful evening was like a warm, comforting hug helping him to get over the stresses of the day.

How he missed having someone to come back to at night, someone who could help put Gracie to bed or to share a glass of wine with as he unwound at the end of a long day. It had been the simple things in a partnership that had often brought him the most joy and he'd forgotten that until he'd come home to Summer.

Her hair had fallen in a golden curtain hiding her face from view when he really needed to see her. He reached out and gently tucked it behind her ear, the slight contact stirring her into a lazy smile.

'Hello, sleepyhead.'

Her green eyes blinked back at him and she scrambled to sit up. 'Sorry, I tried to stay awake. I wanted to make sure you…er…everything was okay.'

She was brushing her tangled hair away from her face and trying to smooth out her crumpled clothes but she looked perfectly adorable the way she was. This tousled vision gave him a glimpse of what she'd look like first thing in the morning and stirred feelings inside him he'd thought he'd never experience again.

If he hadn't been so damaged by his previous relationship he could wake up to her in his bed looking just like this. It was a tempting thought and the conflicting emotions she aroused in him reminded him of the man he was as well as being a surgeon and father. He felt very protective of her when she looked so vulnerable but he also had an urge to kiss her until she was fully awake.

An act that wasn't appropriate when all she'd done was help him out during a very difficult time.

'The operation went well and she's in Recovery. It's going to take a while for her to heal completely and she'll likely have to come back here for rehab, but we've done everything we can for now.'

'I'm glad to hear it.'

'I'm so sorry for keeping you out all night.' He knew he should let her go and get some rest but since Summer was at the heart of a lot of the decisions and emotions he had to work through he appreciated having her with him. Logic and his self-imposed restrictions aside, he enjoyed being with her. With the sound of that crash still ringing in his ears and the what-ifs hounding him, he realised he didn't want to be alone, but he'd already asked so much of her tonight.

'It's not as though you were out partying, Rafael. There was an emergency. I was there, remember? You did what you had to do for that poor family and Gracie and I have been fine.'

'I know, and I'm eternally grateful you stepped up to help without hesitation. I just hate to impose on you, although if she's asleep it does make me feel a little less guilty.' It wouldn't have come as a surprise if Gracie had been howling until he'd come home to tuck her into bed, especially after the shock they'd had. It was comforting to know she'd been able to settle for Summer and it stopped him fretting about working away from his daughter.

'She did fuss for a while that you weren't here to read her a bedtime story and went to bed clutching one of your shirts. I hope that's okay? She took it from your closet and it seemed to give her some comfort.'

'That's fine. We don't really have anyone else to turn to at times like this. Her mother hasn't wanted to know her for the past two years and my parents, well, they kind of disowned me when I left Spain. They don't know who I am these days, much less their granddaughter.'

'It's their loss, on both counts.' It was meant as a compliment but it did make Rafael wonder if it was Gracie's loss, too, that she'd never get to know the rest of her family. He'd been so hurt and determined to succeed without their help that he'd forgotten about what was best for his daughter. She was the innocent party here and though he didn't want her to get hurt there was a possibility he had been projecting his insecurities onto her.

'I try not to dwell on it but today has opened my eyes. What if we had been in that car? What would happen to Gracie if I got hurt, or vice versa? I'm not sure either of us would survive without the other.' He was horrified to hear the slight crack in his voice, showing his one true weakness in front of Summer, but he hadn't planned for that eventuality. If he was ever seriously ill or injured, his daughter would be left at the mercy of children's services because he'd been too afraid to share her with anyone else.

'I'm always here for both of you.' She let her hand rest lightly atop his, a gentle reminder she was there, and he appreciated it more than she would ever know. It was a long time since he'd had that kind of support.

'Thank you. I'm glad she didn't give you too much of a hard time tonight in case I have to take you up on that.' A wrinkled shirt was a small price to pay for peace of mind tonight and now he had assurance that he wasn't on his own any more, everything he'd shared with Summer was worth it.

'Not at all. We were working on some posters for the triathlon idea.' She let go of him and rooted through the mess of paper and colouring utensils littering his coffee table to present him with their joint efforts.

'Well, these masterpieces should have people digging deep into their pockets.' He could just imagine the two of them, heads bent over the table, doing their best to illustrate Summer's ideas, and the image was heart-warming. They'd formed a real bond and he knew that wasn't something achieved easily with his daughter, or him. She was someone special.

'I showed her some of these so she'd understand what it is we're trying to do.' Summer grabbed her cell and came to sit on the arm of the couch beside him, scrolling through to show him a video of a triathlon.

'I'm not sure any of us are quite in that league,' he joked, trying to ignore the warm feel of her pressed against his arm or her hair brushing against his cheek and awakening every nerve ending in his body.

'I thought we could make it an annual event and perhaps make the first one for those hospital staff who are already in shape. Present company included, of course.' Her smile, so warm, so close, sucked all the oxygen from his lungs and it took some time before he was able to respond.

'And you'll be taking part too?'

'Not this time. Perhaps we could run a training course for those of us who need some practice for next year. Gracie even gave me some inspiration for running a nursery triathlon for a bit of fun. Nothing competitive. You know, some water play, trikes and a race, so the children could feel involved too.'

When he didn't reply she shoved the phone back in her pocket. 'It's probably a silly idea anyway...'

Rafael took her hand and laced his fingers through hers to show her he was there for her as she had been for him and Gracie. 'No, it's a great idea. You're amazing.'

'So are you. Gracie couldn't have asked for a better father and the way you dealt with that crash today was incredible.'

They locked eyes and it was then he realised there was more than mutual appreciation going on. He'd let Summer get closer to him than anyone since Christina because that's exactly where he wanted her to be.

'Summer…' Saying her name was an acceptance of his feelings for her that he'd been denying too long.

'Rafael…' She leaned in and as her lips met his in a soft caress, he was lost to the sensation. With the tip of his tongue he traced the outline of her mouth, dipped in to taste her sweetness, but when she gave a breathy moan he was carried away on a tidal wave of need. He shifted her over onto his lap and she made no protest. Instead, she wrapped her arms around his neck and gave herself over to the passion threatening to consume them both.

He hadn't been intimate with any woman since Christina had left but he didn't remember a simple kiss having such power over him, to the point nothing else mattered but maintaining that connection. It was only the thought of Gracie sleeping upstairs that eventually cooled his ardour before they were both swept away in the moment. He dotted kisses along the side of her neck, trying to wean himself away from her in small stages, afraid to break the spell and the possibilities that might be opening up for them.

He was still nursing his wounds from the divorce and he wasn't in the right head space to get involved with anyone. As illustrated by his toing and froing with Summer, unable to tear himself away but knowing he shouldn't get involved.

'Promise you won't hurt me, Rafael.' Summer was so moved by the unexpected kiss and her reaction to it, she knew she was in trouble. So much for her triathlon distraction. When he'd confided in her, showing that vulnerability she hadn't known was there, she'd been transfixed, captivated by his charms. Now she had sampled the evidence that his interest in her went beyond his daughter she would be at his mercy.

'I don't know what this is we're getting into, Summer, but I do have to consider Gracie in whatever happens. What I can promise is that I would never intentionally do anything to hurt you when I've endured that suffering myself. Christina did so much damage to us both when she left, I'm afraid of getting involved and leaving us both exposed to that pain again.'

It was the first time he'd mentioned his ex's name and it somehow made her existence more real, a possible threat. She understood Rafael's reasons for being guarded when her last break-up was the reason she was wary of another single dad. 'I would never hurt either of you. I hope you know that.'

'It's down to my own hang-ups, nothing you've done. Before Christina it was my parents who let me go without a fight. They didn't want me to leave my home country and when I did they saw it as a betrayal of my heritage. I guess I'm just afraid of losing anyone else in my life and I've been using excuses to push you away rather than face what's happening between us. You've been honest with me and I've seen how much you care for Gracie, for everyone in your life.'

'I don't play games, Rafael. I wear my heart on my sleeve. I like you, I want to be with you.' She knew how it felt to be so isolated from people she loved and she could never do that to someone else. He didn't have to worry that she would treat him as badly as his own family had.

'I know.' He leaned in and dropped a soft kiss on her lips to remind her he was still there.

'I couldn't bear to lose anyone else in my life, Rafael. My stepbrother is living goodness knows where with my father, and my ex-boyfriend went back to his previous partner, taking the son I'd helped him raise. Trust me when I say I'm not in the market for any more heartache.'

Rafael brushed away her silent tears with the pads of his thumbs. 'From now on we're only making happy memories.' He sealed the promise with another gentle kiss, so tender it was easy to believe he'd never hurt her.

'Look, I like you, Rafael, and I'm pretty sure you like me.' She touched her finger to her kiss-swollen lips as though she could still feel him. 'Why don't we just leave it at that for now with no expectations or worries about the consequences?'

Goodness knew, she wanted more of this, of

him, but she knew he would never choose her above his daughter, she wouldn't expect him to. Yet a part of her wanted him to fight for her. The part of her that had been cast aside without a second thought when the mother of her ex's baby had come back on the scene as if she'd never been an important piece of his history. Her heart.

He looked surprised when she offered him a way out, and disengaged herself from his lap. 'Summer, I—'

'It's late. I should really get home and get some sleep.' She couldn't bear to hear empty promises when he'd probably come to regret this in the morning.

'It doesn't seem very gentlemanly of me to let you walk home alone.' He stood beside her, his ruffled hair and dazed expression a reminder of the passion they'd just shared.

Summer shook her head. 'I wouldn't expect you to when you have Gracie to look after.'

She left Rafael's house more confused than ever about how to proceed with him, knowing she'd shown her hand tonight. The life she'd created here for herself was a sign she deserved more than being a mere stop-gap in someone else's love life. Maple Island was her home now. She was happy in her job and at peace with the decisions that had brought her here because she knew now that Marc hadn't been the right man for her.

That kiss with Rafael had been an expression of the depth of her feelings for him, and having experienced the strength of his intoxicating passion in return had left her feeling weak. She was falling for him fast and she didn't know where that left her if he decided he didn't want her after all. She wasn't a book from the library to be borrowed and put back on the shelf at will, and cursed herself for getting involved with another man with complicated family issues.

'Wake up, Papa.'

Rafael's fevered dreams about kissing Summer were quickly doused as he was slapped awake by his three-year-old.

'Wh-what time is it?' He reached for his watch on the nightstand, trying to force himself awake in case he'd overslept again. Given last night's events, he wouldn't have been surprised. He and Summer had crossed the line into romantic territory and he still had to process exactly what that meant for him, and Gracie.

His effective alarm call climbed down off his bed and toddled off out of the room again. As the numbers came into focus, he groaned and lay back down on the pillow. It was way too early for this.

'Go back to bed, Gracie.' He closed his eyes, grateful he had another couple of hours before he really had to get up. Unfortunately, the sound of cupboards being opened downstairs in the kitchen and the sound of dishes breaking ensured he was jumping out of bed seconds later.

Apparently, she was big and smart enough that safety gates and cupboard locks no longer posed any threat, except to his mental health. There were so many potential dangers he bounded down the staircase without a thought to the hazards of being barefoot.

After finding the plastic building blocks

she'd abandoned on the floor, he hopped into a scene of utter carnage in the kitchen.

'Are you okay?' Ignoring the trail of cereal across the floor and the milk waterfall currently pouring off the kitchen worktop, he was more concerned with the damage she could've done to herself.

'Breakfast, Papa.' She was so pleased with herself as she presented him with a half-full glass of orange juice and a bowl of soggy cereal, there was no way he could be cross with her. He could clear the mess up any time but it wasn't often his daughter did something so amazing for him.

'*Gracias, querida.*' He kissed the top of her head, tears springing to his eyes that she would even think of trying to make breakfast for him. It wasn't yet clear to what extent her autism would impact on her life when she was older, but this small act was a welcome sign she was aware of the world around her and was capable of displaying emotion. If this wasn't an expression of a child's love for her father, he didn't know what was.

He poured her some orange juice and cereal

and pulled out a chair for her to join him. 'Did you have fun last night?'

She nodded whilst munching a mouthful of multigrain hoops and he decided to push a little further when she was being this co-operative.

'You like Summer, don't you?'

She gave another emphatic nod as she shovelled in another spoonful of cereal.

'Yeah, me too. We're going to be working on this triathlon together so you don't mind if she comes around sometimes?' It was true, even if he hoped she'd be here for other reasons too. He wanted Gracie to be happy with the idea before he would even contemplate getting in deeper with Summer.

This time she shook her head and Rafael ate the breakfast prepared by his daughter with a smile on his face. Sitting here in the midst of this chaos, puddles of juice, milk and cereal covering every available surface, it was the best meal he'd ever had.

As Summer made her way to Rafael's house, she knew the decision had been made on what part she was to play in his life. The invitation to join him and Gracie for dinner had been a personal one and not offered in any professional capacity. Still, she'd brought along all the stuff she'd been working on for the triathlon. It mightn't have done anything to stop their burgeoning attraction to one another but it would benefit the clinic nonetheless.

She worried that he would have had time to think about last night and regret kissing her, but he'd arrived at day-care this morning so eager to tell her what Gracie had done for him at breakfast it was clear he wanted her to be a part of their lives.

It was a leap of faith for both of them to begin a relationship, even if they'd been involved long before either of them had admitted it. If she left all thoughts of Marc and Leo in the past and simply let herself live in the moment, she knew she had to take the chance she could be happy.

'Hey.' She had to resist throwing herself at Rafael as he opened the door to let her in, so sexy in his charcoal-grey T-shirt and tight black jeans. Somehow his casual look did more for her than his dapper formal wear or the scrubs she knew a lot of women found attractive. Perhaps it was the novelty of seeing him relaxed or the hungry look in his eyes she knew was for more than food. Either way, he certainly didn't need to serve aphrodisiacs tonight to get her attention.

'Hey, yourself.' He closed the door, backing her up against it, and kissed her with such fiery passion she was sure her bones had melted.

She'd barely recovered by the time he led her to the dining room where she flopped into a chair. Her body was so weakened from that one kiss she daren't think about what else he could do to her or she might combust with want.

'Dinner smells lovely.' She took a sip of the wine he'd poured for her, hoping the alcohol would revive her from her swoon.

'Gracie helped me make the *patatas bravas*. I hope you're hungry.' Rafael set the dish of cubed potatoes in spicy tomato sauce beside the tray of herbed chicken and vegetables in the middle of the table so they could help themselves. Though her insides were fluttering in anticipation of the night that lay ahead, Summer tucked in along with father and daughter.

She enjoyed sharing dinner with them. It had been so long since she'd sat down to a family meal she'd forgotten what it was like to chat and swap stories of their day. The simple conversation and companionship was what she'd missed most when Leo and Marc had vanished from her life because they'd been the only ones to provide it since her own parents had split. Although she was afraid to get too used to it in case the same thing happened again, it was good to feel part of a family once more.

Once Gracie started yawning, both she and Rafael teamed up again to get her to bed. It was a routine the little girl seemed to accept, even with Summer there, and it wasn't difficult to imagine this could be something long term. The thought of that was holding more appeal by the second.

CHAPTER SEVEN

THEY LAUNCHED AT each other the second they closed Gracie's bedroom door. With her arms draped around his neck, Summer surrendered herself to Rafael's touch and he took immediate possession. He tangled his hands in her hair as his lips moved across hers, his genuine feelings for her there in the urgency of his kiss.

The cyclone of lust twisting their bodies around one another was in danger of whisking them off to the fantasy land where this was possible.

'Where's your room?'

Rafael questioned her decision with a raised eyebrow but she was a woman who knew exactly what she wanted.

He took her by the hand and led her to the room at the end of the hallway, kicking the door shut behind them before reclaiming her with his arms and lips. His kisses were every bit as confident and sexy as she'd been recalling all day, apparently without exaggeration. Now they were alone and free to express the desire that had been building since last night, clothes seemed an unnecessary hindrance, although it had been a while since she'd slept with a man and admitted as much to him, so there was no confusion about the significance of what they were about to embark upon together.

'I…er…haven't done this for a while.' She was gulping feverishly as he kissed his way down her neck, opening the buttons on her shirt to follow the path into the valley of her cleavage.

He briefly paused his expedition to give her a smirk. 'Neither have I, Summer. I'm sure we can help each other remember what we're supposed to be doing.' The glint in his eye sent shivers of delight rippling across her skin and he continued to strip her while covering her in hot, sensual kisses.

By the time she was clad only in her underwear she didn't care about anything other than soothing that ache for him within. He slid the straps of her bra excruciatingly slowly down her arms, undid the clasp and let her breasts spill free. The shock of the air on her skin puckered her nipples and she gasped when his mouth found them.

'Rafael...' She was on the brink of incapacitating ecstasy, pleading for release when she hadn't even touched him or undressed him in return.

'I'm enjoying getting acquainted with you. If it's okay with you, I'd prefer to take my time.' Even in the dark she could tell he was grinning, relishing the fact that he'd rendered her speechless.

'Uh-huh.' She closed her eyes and left her body at his mercy.

He hooked his fingers inside her panties, slowly drew them down her legs and proceeded to trail his tongue down the centre of her torso until she was naked and he was kneeling at her feet.

She was breathless with want as his hot breath skimmed over her inner thighs and he teased her open with the tip of his tongue. Her legs were trembling as he plunged deep inside her wet core, lapping the arousal about to consume her whole. She held onto his shoulders for support as he continued to drive her closer to the edge of oblivion.

With his hands squeezing her buttocks, his tongue a swirling tornado inside her, he whipped her into a frenzy of lust. His relentless quest for her orgasm sent her spiralling much quicker than she'd ever believed possible. She shuddered again and again, every aftershock of her climax leaving her limbs quivering with the effort of holding her upright.

Once Rafael had rendered her completely incapable of speech and mobility, he established control of her ragdoll body and carried her towards the bed. Although she'd have been happy to divest him of his clothes, she was equally content to watch him do the job himself, revealing the physique she'd been drooling over ever since he'd arrived on the island.

The evidence of all his sporting prowess was there in every toned, tanned inch of taut muscle, although his most impressive body part had been gifted to him by Mother Nature. Summer considered herself a very lucky woman indeed.

The way she was unashamedly staring at his naked form, her eyes dark with desire, was hardening him even more than bringing her to climax with his mouth alone. She made him feel wanted, desirable in a way he hadn't experienced since Graciela had been born.

She was lying here beneath him, beautifully exposed for his appreciation and panting with want for him, and he was going to savour every second. He slid slowly between her soft thighs into that slick, tight heat that made him jerk and almost abandon his vow. His groan chorused with Summer's as they finally forged that connection they'd been afraid of from the start.

Once past that initial, brief resistance as she adjusted to him inside her, Rafael began to move, both of them voicing their pleasure with every thrust and making a mystery of why they'd waited so long for this. Sex had always been about more than the physical act for him. For him the act was the culmination of his feelings for someone, not the starting point, and he wouldn't be here with Summer if he didn't believe she was someone special in his life.

He knew it was the same for her when she'd confided in him about how much her ex had hurt her. There was no way she'd have rushed into this with him based on lust alone, even if it felt like that when she was digging her nails into his backside and urging him deeper inside her. She was making it difficult for him to prolong their mutual satisfaction when she was sucking his earlobe into her mouth and grinding her pelvis into his.

His head was pounding with the rush of blood and endorphins coursing through his veins at breakneck speed. She leaned into him, her breath in his ear causing the pressure in his loins to build until he was no longer able to contain it. Then she contracted her inner muscles around his shaft and the dam burst in a spectacular roar.

He poured everything he had into her and with the last strokes of his climax he carried her there again with him.

They clung together, sweat glistening on

their skin, chests heaving with the effort of breathing, and Rafael couldn't wipe the grin from his face. She was as amazing as he'd been afraid of because he knew he'd never want to leave her bed again.

When they finally extricated themselves from one another, bodies limp and breathing laboured, it was Summer who spoke first. She only managed one word but one that echoed his own thoughts.

'Wow!'

He rested his hand on his chest, feeling his heart beating fast and clear and making him feel more alive than he had since Christina had left, when he'd thought his whole world had ended. It was a reminder he still had a right to a life of his own outside his role of a parent. Not only was he a father and a surgeon but he was also a red-blooded man with his own loves and wants and he should no longer be content to set them aside.

He was almost afraid to recognise his current mood for fear of jinxing it but as he lay in the afterglow of their lovemaking he was content. Maple Island had provided him with a home, a job, a safe community for his daughter and a partner with whom he hoped to share all aspects of his life.

He turned onto his side but found himself too choked up to tell her how much she meant to him so he showed her with a kiss. Her lips were reciprocating all those emotions that went beyond great sex.

For what seemed the longest time they lay staring into one another's eyes, only breaking eye contact every now and then to indulge in some more sensual caresses and generally making the most of the little world they'd created for themselves in this room.

He smoothed the flat of his hand over the contours of Summer's body, mesmerised by her curves as his hand dipped in at the indent at her waist and over the flare of her hips, and wishing they never had to don clothes again.

'I'll have to leave before Gracie sees me.' Summer reminded him he had responsibilities beyond his libido and it showed how much she cared about his daughter that she even raised the subject.

'There's still plenty of time before she wakes.'

He wouldn't want to upset his little girl by finding a woman in his bed but he'd give anything to be able to fall asleep here for the night with Summer in his arms.

She nodded to show her understanding of his situation but the worrying of her bottom lip with her teeth showed she didn't want to leave either.

Rafael didn't want to treat Summer as second best to his daughter but there would have to be a gentle lead in to their relationship around her. It would require specialist juggling skills to balance family duties with his love life now that he might have one.

Summer's selfless attitude and empathy for Gracie was the sort of unconditional love and understanding a mother should have. She would never expect him to choose between them, jealous of the attention he devoted to his daughter, but neither did he wish to confine her to the shadows.

'You know I'll be accompanying Paisley on her transfer to Boston?' She'd needed some time to recover from her operation but tomorrow they'd be moving her to the mainland. A gem of an idea had shone in his thoughts as he'd searched for a way to combine his time with those most precious to him without upsetting anyone. It would be impossible, not to mention painful, to expect the woman in his life to remain at arm's length now.

'Hmm…' She eyed him with caution but he wanted a concrete plan in place to see each other again.

'Why don't you and Gracie come over on the ferry and we'll spend some time in the city together?'

Her eyes grew wide at the suggestion and her ensuing response would surely set the tone for the continuing nature of their relationship.

Summer knew this was a big deal and in some ways a greater step forward for them than sleeping together. Although that had been spectacular in itself and she was thoroughly satiated from the experience.

Spending the day with Gracie, being given sole responsibility for her welfare and getting her to the city was a sign of Rafael's trust in her. A decision he would not take lightly when he'd spent so long trying to protect her from outside influences.

However, she didn't want his sudden keenness to integrate her into their family life to override everything else. Not only was it going to be a difficult transition for Gracie to get used to seeing her in a more personal capacity but Summer had a position at the clinic that extended beyond one adorable child and her delectable dad.

'Isn't that a lot to expect from Gracie at such short notice?' Summer could rise to the challenge if they were all in agreement but it could prove a step too far for Gracie to take her out of nursery to embark on a trip without her father.

'I know I can count on you to take care of her and I'm sure she'll love the idea of visiting Boston again.' That level of faith in her when he'd fought against her for so long raised goosebumps along her skin. She knew it came from more than sharing a bed but she couldn't help but think it was such a turnaround he could be making rash decisions based on his current euphoria. It also dragged her further into their family dynamic and she was afraid that would lead to more hurt if it all went wrong and she lost that mothering role to Gracie as well as being Rafael's partner. She'd be the one left with the gaping hole in her heart when he'd still have his daughter.

'What about nursery or, you know, my job? I can't just call in and inform them I'm taking the day off so I can play hooky with you.' It was what she wanted to do but she had to be an adult about this. Her position at the clinic was important to her and she wasn't about to blow it off simply for that first flush of excitement that came with a new relationship.

'Alex and Cody have asked me to be in that helicopter. I'll tell them I don't want to leave Gracie and you're the only one who can bring her across, which is all true. I'm sure the clinic can manage without us for one day.'

There was more chance of him swinging her the day off when his position here was superior to hers. 'I suppose one day off isn't going to kill me, or anyone else.'

'Our patients will still be here when we get back and there are plenty of staff to take care of them in our absence. That is, if the idea of spending the day with us appeals to you? I wouldn't want to railroad you into agreeing.'

'I'd love to spend time with you and Gracie away from here. I just don't want to jeopardise my job in the process.'

'I would never ask you to do that, Summer. I promise I'll sort out the details first thing but it's important you know I'd never force these decisions on you. You will always be free to do whatever you're comfortable with. Including if you decide to walk away.' All the tension was back in his face, his jaw clenched, frown lines running across his forehead and his brown eyes almost black with the sincerity he was expressing to her.

He couldn't have been any clearer that he wasn't pressuring her and that she should want to be with them by her own volition. She could only imagine the burden of guilt he'd endured in the aftermath of his divorce if his ex had made him feel as though they'd been lead weights dragging her down.

'There is nowhere I'd rather be. Well, maybe one other place.'

She snuggled her naked body closer into his and hoped the morning wouldn't come too quickly when she'd have to sneak away before she was spotted.

'No Dolly.' Gracie lifted the doll Summer had been using to try and persuade her to get into the car and threw it on the ground.

They'd both spoken to Gracie about their plans, omitting any reference to personal developments. It had been a mutual decision not to rush her into the middle of that until she'd had time to get used to Summer sharing her father. Otherwise it would be overwhelming for her to accept that her nursery teacher was kissing Daddy.

He'd kissed them both—his passionate embrace with Summer out of sight from impressionable young eyes—and set off for his helicopter transfer to Boston. Now, realising she was expected to get into a strange car and leave the island without her father, Gracie was understandably distressed.

The important thing was for Summer to remain calm and not get hung up on Rafael waiting for them. Gracie would pick up on her stress and it wouldn't get them on the ferry any quicker. What this would take was patience, reassurance and some ingenuity.

'That's a shame.' Summer brushed out Dolly's wool hair and Gracie turned down the volume of her screaming. 'Dolly was looking forward to her day out at the aquarium seeing the fish. She was hoping to make some new friends too.'

Curiosity shifted Gracie's focus from the absence of her father to the doll in Summer's hand. Summer waited patiently, silently with the car door open and let the child believe this decision was hers alone. After a time Gracie snatched back ownership of Dolly and climbed into the back seat with her.

Once both were safely belted into the car, Gracie's buggy loaded into the trunk in case her sprained ankle became too painful to walk on, Summer let out a long, steady breath. It was entirely different managing a child with challenging needs in a controlled environment such as the clinic or the nursery compared to out in the real world. She had no authority, no current support or even a right to be here. This was Gracie's world and Summer would have to adjust in order to fit in.

Rafael had been right to be cautious when it came to their relationship. A casual affair would never work when he was devoted to Gracie and anyone he got involved with would have to be equally as dedicated. Not all women would be prepared to take on the responsibilities she represented. Thankfully Summer had already formed an attachment to the little girl and was honoured Rafael had acknowledged that by inviting her further into their lives.

Although it was a tad daunting when she'd been here before with Marc and her bruised heart should've been a reminder to maintain some detachment. Impossible when she'd already fallen for the two brown-eyed beauties. She would never comprehend Christina's decision to leave her lovely family behind when they'd already become such a big part of her life in a relatively short space of time.

The calm crossing and long drive lulled Gracie to sleep for the duration of the journey so there were no more dramas between Maple Island and Boston.

The hustle and bustle of the city she'd been raised in came as a shock to the system after the sedate nature of island life she'd become accustomed to. Being plunged back into sensory overload with the bright lights and noise of city life could have an adverse effect on Gracie too. Rafael had commented on how the slower pace on Maple Island had lessened the frequency of her outbursts so it was a concern the reverse could happen back in Boston.

Although he'd taken that into consideration given the itinerary he'd planned, meeting them at the aquarium where Gracie would find some relief from the crowds on the bustling streets.

The guilt about taking time off at short notice to play happy families hadn't left her, even though Rafael had apparently smoothed it over with the big bosses. Perhaps it was because her job had become her whole life since leaving the mainland, the only relationship she'd had since Marc, and she was cheating on it with Rafael and Gracie. They were claiming huge chunks of her time and her heart, moving her away from being a workaholic avoiding emotional entanglements back into a fully functioning human being who was starting to think she could have it all.

Her phone buzzed with a message from Rafael.

I'll be there soon. Missing you. Xx

Every letter broadened the smile on her face further, knowing they'd be reunited shortly, he was missing her and sending virtual kisses, making her feel as giddy as a teenager with her first love.

'Good news, Gracie, your father is going to be with us soon.'

Gracie giggled, her attention elsewhere as the stingray came to the surface of the touch tank to let her stroke him. Every now and then he splashed some water over the edge of the tank onto her shoes, making her laugh like Summer had never heard before.

'I think he likes you.' The feeling was mutual, as illustrated by the inordinate amount of time they'd spent here, but Gracie was in her element. She'd been enamoured by all the exhibits and an absolute joy to be around. It was a shame Rafael had missed this part of the day but she'd taken plenty of photographs to mark the occasion. If it wasn't too far out of her jurisdiction she might suggest he get a pet for Gracie when she was as engaged as this.

'You two seem to be having fun together.' Rafael's voice, low in her ear, coupled with his arms sliding around her waist, made Summer every bit as happy as their budding marine biologist.

She kept her eyes on Gracie as Rafael kissed her neck and once she was sure they wouldn't be spotted she spun around to give him a much-too-quick peck hello.

'So far, so good.' It wouldn't do any good to recount the blip they'd had this morning before boarding the ferry when it was the same trying to get any small child to comply and she didn't want to spoil the rest of the day by mentioning any problems to him.

'*Hola*, Graciela.' He moved towards his daughter and she rewarded him with a toothy grin and sticking his hand in the cold water to meet her new friend.

'I think you could have trouble if you try to get her to leave. Her fingers will be wrinkled by now they've spent so long in there.' Neither of them minded when she was enjoying herself but Summer was looking forward to whatever else Rafael had in store for them today.

'That would be a shame when I'd planned another trip for us.' He spoke loud enough for Gracie to hear and she sidled closer around the perimeter of the tank to listen.

'I guess we'll just have to stay here until closing time.' Summer huffed out a sigh and played along.

'We'll save the boat trip to see the whales for the next time.'

Now she would be genuinely gutted if they couldn't go. It had been years since she'd gone whale watching and there was no one she'd rather share the experience with than current company.

The prospect of more sea life proved irresistible to an inquisitive three-year-old and she eventually whispered goodbye to the stingray and presented her wet palms to her father.

'I think this means she's ready to go.' He laughed and dried her off with the paper towels provided for the ray-whisperers.

Summer held out a hand and Gracie slid her fingers in to interlace with hers and grabbed her father with the other hand so the three of them strolled through the halls of the aquarium all linked together.

The transition from the clinic to Boston Harbour Hospital had been as straightforward as the team could've expected. Once Rafael was sure the patient was comfortable he'd hardly been able to wait to reunite with Gracie and Summer.

Nothing ever ran to plan with a child on the autistic spectrum and those not used to his daughter's *quirks* were often stressed at the end of their time with her. It hadn't been a test when Summer had previous experience with her but he was able to relax once he'd seen for himself how well they'd managed without him. There were bound to have been some hiccups along the way but Summer apparently didn't deem them significant enough to mention.

It was great for him to be able to delegate some of that responsibility and not be obligated to apologise or gush thanks for it but it would take some getting used to. For the duration of Gracie's young life so far he'd made every decision on her behalf, decreed he was to be consulted night and day on anything affecting his daughter, and it was a huge step to believe that Summer could manage without his input. He'd entrusted the most precious thing in his life to her and that wasn't something he did without considerable thought. It was a decision he'd taken in order for them to progress in their relationship and show her he was opening up his heart and his family because she was so special to him.

He'd have been devastated if Summer had declared she'd had enough after trying to wrangle Gracie on the journey, and would've spelled the end of the affair. There wouldn't have been any point in continuing if she couldn't accommodate his daughter and vice versa because there was no alternative available. He had no intention of embarking on a fling because it would be impossible to divide his time so completely between a partner and his family, even if he'd only been after a physical affair. He wasn't, of course, he was enjoying Summer's company, especially as she understood them better than anyone else ever had.

Deep down he hadn't expected her to let them down because he'd never have left Gracie in her care if he'd imagined she couldn't cope. Now he had definitive proof he could throw off the shackles of the past and live in the moment with both of them.

'Are you cold, *querida niña*?' Despite the appropriate layers of clothing they'd donned in preparation for their whale watching, Gracie wasn't always able to communicate to him if she was too cold.

'I can take you downstairs where it's warmer,' Summer offered, but Gracie clung tighter to the side of the catamaran, content to wait it out for the promised whale sighting.

The boat lurched on the choppy sea along with his stomach. For all his planning he hadn't figured motion sickness into the equation.

'How are you doing?' The gentle hand rubbing his back as he leaned over the rail was as comforting as the sound of her sympathetic words.

He couldn't remember the last time anyone asked him about his well-being. That warm glow inside that it gave him knowing someone cared immediately improved his condition.

'I'm fine. I wouldn't miss this for the world,' he said, hoping she realised that every time he took her hand, in his head he was kissing her. Hand-holding had suddenly become acceptable in Gracie's eyes, alternating between him and Summer, sometimes clinging to both, other times insisting he and Summer held hands too.

He didn't know what had brought this on other than it being a sign she was comfortable in the company of both adults and accepting their intimacy at hand-holding level. It was more than he'd expected but it was a positive boost for the bonds they were attempting to forge.

Summer responded with a squeeze that he chose to interpret as a lingering embrace. His pleasure at being close to her was matched by the joy of seeing and hearing his daughter pointing and shrieking at everything that came into view. From the harbour seal they passed, to the squawking gannets who'd swooped down to plunder his freshly caught fish and the frequent bombardment of gulls, she'd cherished every sighting. Both he and Summer took time to educate her on the species she spied while they had her attention.

'I think we'll have to do this more often. I mean if you want to, or it could be something you and Gracie might prefer to do on your own.' Her assumption she'd be joining them on another family outing made him smile just as much as her attempt to take it back. She was already thinking of them as a unit and he didn't mind a bit.

'We will have to do it again. All three of us.'

She stopped rambling once he assured her she was welcome to join them any time. It made trips out fun for him as well as Gracie to have someone there he could have an adult conversation with and share the experience. Until Summer had entered his life he hadn't realised how lonely and empty his life was outside work and fatherhood. He had nothing of his own.

She lived up to her name, bright and sunny, lighting up the world around her when it was needed most. Rafael stepped in between the two females in his life and put his arms around them, making precious memories to last for ever.

All at once a chorus of shrieks went up around him.

'Look out there.'

He followed Summer's instruction and spotted a whale, which the on-board naturalist informed them was the elusive, and critically endangered, North Atlantic whale.

Further out in the water a humpback cast its fluke to wave as they passed. The amazing sights left them all spellbound. Watching Summer's eyes sparkle and cheeks flush with every new visitor was as exhilarating as the brisk wind and the glories of nature.

Some of the whales performed synchronised diving for their audience, drawing applause from the passengers. They soon had another species vying for their attention as a group of Atlantic white-sided dolphins began leaping in and out of the sea and showing off for anyone present. They captivated one particular fan.

'Oh, Rafael. They're beautiful. This is the best day of my life.' Summer clapped her appreciation for their acrobatic display, her enthusiasm mirrored by Gracie, who was holding up her doll so she could watch too.

Even with such a wondrous visual feast before him, Rafael was still drawn back to the face of the woman beside him, so excited by the spectacle she was in danger of bursting.

'Mine too,' he whispered, and felt her quiver beneath his touch. He was looking forward to some quality alone time with her once Gracie was in bed.

On their return to the harbour it became clear the fresh air had caught up with the youngest member of their party as she dragged her feet about getting off the boat again.

'We can't leave you here overnight, you'll freeze.' Summer tried to coax her into her pushchair as the rest of the other passengers disembarked. They'd waited until the rush to the exit had subsided in case the crush proved too much but Gracie was equally uncooperative on the almost empty vessel. His daughter's response was to stamp her feet, throw Dolly at Summer and refuse to budge.

That lightness Rafael had been experiencing dissipated, his body grounded once more by the prospect of one of Gracie's epic tantrums. It wasn't that he got embarrassed or that he wasn't used to dealing with them but because every time she displayed traits of her condition he worried it would cause Summer to have second thoughts about what she was getting into with them. Even though she'd been nothing but supportive so far.

'Gracie, we've got to get off so we can go home. You want to get back to Maple Island, don't you?' He tried to physically move her but that only resulted in further screaming and his shins taking a few well-aimed kicks from his surprisingly strong daughter.

Unfortunately, her meltdowns didn't run to any typical schedule and there was no way of predicting how long this would last or to what extremes her temper would reach. All anyone could do was let her work through it until she was ready to move on. That was difficult to explain to strangers, or those not sympathetic to the condition, who thought this behaviour was down to bad parenting. Summer might understand the circumstances better than most but it didn't make it any easier to live with.

When Gracie reached the stage of jumping on and off the seats, Summer simply took a seat on deck and waited with him for her to tire herself out.

The boat captain appeared and tutted. 'We have another party due to leave soon.'

It was Summer who tackled him on Gracie's behalf. 'I understand that, sir, but if you could leave us for a few minutes we'd have a much better chance of getting her to co-operate.'

The man screwed his face up in disapproval before turning on his heel and walking away.

Rafael was impressed with Summer's defence of his daughter and her acceptance of the situation as if it was the norm. It was a relief to have someone on their side, who wore her heart and her allegiance to his family for the world to see. She had their backs and he was thankful that he no longer had to do this alone any more. With her they were no longer outsiders pushed out to the peripheries of existence but very much participants who deserved their place alongside everyone else.

It was this unconditional support from her that eased open the final latch on his heart. Summer was the one and only person he knew he could trust with that fragile part of him when she'd proved time and again she loved his family as much as he did. He wanted a future with her in it and he could only truly have that if he gave everything of himself to her. Once they got home he would make sure she knew how strongly he felt about her and stop holding back because of what had happened in the past. She wasn't Christina, she was Summer, who had been there for him and Gracie since the day they'd met.

With the certainty she wasn't going to be put off by these outbursts from time to time, he took a leaf out of her book and reacted as though what was going on around him was perfectly normal. Well, it was for him, it was the rest of the world that had to get used to it and make exceptions for those who didn't fit perfectly into the norms of society.

He and Summer continued discussing everyday topics like what they were having for dinner and what time they'd make it home to Maple Island as though they were any other family. Something he'd thought he'd never have again.

Once Graciela had exhausted herself she climbed into her buggy of her own accord, as Summer had expected she would, eventually.

This time spent with Rafael and Gracie had reminded her how much she enjoyed being part of a family unit. That sense of belonging and feeling complete only came for her when she was with them. Even on the rare occasions she ventured home to visit her mom it left her with the same emptiness inside she'd had when half of her family had been taken away from her. Without her brother and her father in her life she'd thought she'd never find that missing part of her again. Marc and Leo had filled that gap for a while but in hindsight that might have been what had attracted her to him in the first place—a ready-made family who'd taken her in and let her play make-believe.

This was different. Past mistakes should have made her steer clear of Rafael, but if today had shown her anything it was that she genuinely cared for him. She wanted to be with him and Gracie for no other reason than who they were and what they meant to her. They certainly hadn't been looking for a replacement wife and mother any more than she'd been planning on getting involved in someone else's complicated family matters. It had just happened and now she was content to let fate do its thing when it seemed to know better than she did what would make her happy. Apparently, that was no longer hiding away from a life outside her job.

Rafael insisted on one last stop before they left to catch the ferry. 'I know how much you loved the rays, Gracie. Why don't we go to the gift shop and see if we can find a new friend for Dolly?'

'You go on ahead and we'll wait outside. It's pretty busy in there.'

'If you're sure?' He didn't wait for a reply

but simply kissed her on the cheek and disappeared into the aisles of souvenirs and novelty gifts.

Summer turned Gracie's pushchair away from the shop so she didn't notice him slipping away and took a seat opposite the entrance. It was easy to keep track of him as his dark head bobbed above the throng of tourists eager to spend their money. She watched his progress across the floor towards the cash registers as he wasted no time in selecting his purchases. The next time she glanced up the crowd had thinned out and Rafael was deep in animated conversation with a glamorous, dark-haired woman.

He walked away scowling but the stranger tugged his arm, urging him back. It was clear she knew him and though Summer was aware he'd had a life before Maple Island it was a slap in the face to be reminded of it. Seeing him with someone else, despite his reluctance to be engaged in conversation, made her realise it was the strength of her own feelings for him that made it so painful to watch.

She'd fallen for him and couldn't bear to

think of having to share him with anyone except his three-year-old sweetheart. It was impossible to change his past any more than she could her own and she had to accept he had exes out in the world. However, Rafael was different from Marc and committed himself whole-heartedly to everything important to him. She had to believe she was included in that list and he wouldn't be so cavalier about her feelings as to cast her aside as she had been in the past, or she would never be able to move forward with him.

'Time to go,' Rafael said on his return, putting a protective arm around her and propelling them all towards the exit in a hurry.

'Who was that? Is something wrong?' Of course, Summer had witnessed his run-in, she missed nothing, but he refused to let anything ruin their day.

'I'll tell you later. Let's go home.' If Summer had any further questions she didn't raise them. Not that he gave her much of a chance he was in such a rush to get back to the island, away from the ghosts of relationships past, but he didn't want to discuss it in front of Gracie.

Seeing his ex-wife in Boston had been a shock, and a nasty one at that. There might have been a time when he would've been pleased to see her, begged her to come back and try again, but not now. Gracie was his family and Summer was a bigger part of her life than her mother had ever managed.

Given the choice, he'd have preferred never to have set eyes on Christina again. One brief moment back in his life and she'd already wedged herself firmly between him and Summer. The secret of her identity made the silence on their journey home unbearable.

CHAPTER EIGHT

'HOME, SWEET HOME,' Summer declared as she pulled up outside Rafael's house, the engine still running making it clear she wouldn't be staying.

It was his fault things had cooled off between them. Or Christina's, actually. Up until then he and Summer had been closer than ever and now, with Gracie accepting her presence on a personal level, it gave him hope for their future together. That could be in jeopardy if her mother came back on the scene and he wasn't prepared to lose Summer when he'd only just found her.

'Why don't you come in and we'll have a coffee or a nightcap after I get Gracie settled?' He didn't know if, or how, to broach the subject of his ex-wife but he was sure he didn't want their relationship to suffer as a result.

Summer had gone out of her way for the two of them and proved her commitment beyond a doubt. She deserved an explanation, or at least some display of gratitude for everything she'd done today. If Christina hadn't spoiled things they'd have ended the perfect day cuddled up enjoying some quality time together.

'Is that what you want?' Her question was so full of uncertainty it killed him after their day together should've cemented her position in his life, not made her doubt it.

'Yes.' He hoped that definite answer would assure her things remained on track for them. Whatever was going on with Christina had absolutely nothing to do with Summer and she shouldn't be tainted by it.

Once he'd convinced her to stay she parked the car and followed him and Gracie into the house. The fresh air and excitement had caught up with his little whirlwind who, for once, put up no resistance at bedtime so he could put her pyjamas on her with minimal fuss. The only obstacle in getting her settled was when she insisted Summer tuck her into bed.

After reading her a quick bedtime story, Summer made sure she had Dolly in beside her to keep her company. 'Is there anything else I can do for you, Gracie?'

'Can we have a sleepover?' Gracie's request came out of the blue and Rafael wasn't sure she knew what it was she was asking.

'What do you mean, sweetheart?' The room was too compact to host any guests other than her cuddly toys.

'Can Summer stay?' It dawned on him then that she'd enjoyed the novelty of having a woman around. Summer stopped fixing the bed covers, looking to him for some guidance on the issue. Gracie had accepted her so readily, moving their relationship forward much quicker than he'd expected, he had to be certain Summer was comfortable with it too.

'Summer has her own house to go home to and I'm sure she's tired, but she's very welcome to stay. I'd really like that.' He tossed the final decision back to her, making her know he was keen on the idea himself and this wasn't simply Gracie's fancy.

'Will you be here for breakfast?' Gracie

yawned, forcing herself to stay awake until she got the answer she was waiting to hear.

'I…er…' Summer looked towards him again but this had to be her call. If she stayed the night it had to be because she wanted to, not because she'd been pressured into it.

'I make a mean omelette.' He added another incentive in case she'd be more tempted with the offer of food too.

'In that case, how can I resist? I'll be here when you wake up, Gracie.' She kissed her newest admirer on the forehead and when she locked eyes with Rafael he felt the heat of desire flare between them, the night full of possibilities.

'Goodnight, Graciela.' Rafael kissed his daughter too and she made no objection tonight as he exited the room and closed the door.

'Are you sure it's all right for me to stay?' Summer whispered when they were alone in the hallway.

It had been way too long since he'd been able to hold her the way he'd longed to so he gathered her in his arms and took his time answering her with a slow, sensual kiss.

'I'll take that as a yes,' she said with a laugh once they took a breath.

'Thank you for today. You're a very special lady, Summer Ryan.' Now he had her in his life, he didn't intend to lose her.

'Don't you forget it,' she said, poking a finger into his chest.

Regardless of her playfulness now, her usual chatter had been MIA since leaving Boston and he could tell she was bothered by what she'd witnessed earlier.

'The woman in the shop was Christina, my ex-wife.' He didn't want his ex to have any place in their lives but Summer deserved the truth. The colour drained from her face and this was exactly why he hadn't wanted to tell her.

'I see. What did she want?' Although she sounded calm, the news must have come as a huge shock. If she ever ran into her ex he knew he'd find it difficult to be the outsider when they'd had a whole life together he knew little about.

'I didn't give her a chance to say whatever was on her mind. She suggested going somewhere to talk but I didn't want her to see Gracie. So I did the only thing I could think of in the moment. I handed her my business card and told her to call me, to get rid of her.' Her sudden reappearance had cast up all sorts of negative emotions he wasn't ready or willing to revisit, and he wouldn't have gone with her even if he'd been there alone. It hadn't been the time or the place for a confrontation when he wouldn't have been able to stop himself telling her some home truths about what he thought of her for deserting them.

'She must want to see her daughter. Why else would she need to talk to you?'

'She hasn't felt the need to do either for two years. Not even when the divorce papers were served.' He'd long since got over the upset and Gracie didn't remember her at all. All he was bothered about was the impact this was going to have on the life he'd made for himself now with his daughter and Summer.

'Do you…do you think she wants custody?' Summer broached the subject he'd been in denial about ever since he'd crossed paths with Christina today.

'Over my dead body. She isn't a mother to Graciela. She is nothing to her.'

'You'll have to consider that possibility, Rafael. Perhaps she's had a crisis of conscience and decided to make it up to you both. People change.'

'Not in Christina's case. I think she's simply seen me in Boston and tried to stir up trouble. We shouldn't waste any more time thinking about her. I just didn't want to keep any secrets from you. There mightn't be any reason to get worked up anyway when she isn't known for her reliability.' He'd spent too long second-guessing Christina's actions and for the sake of his sanity he'd learned to detach himself from the decisions she made when they were out of control. If he let today's encounter dominate his thoughts he'd go mad at the potential threat she posed to his status quo here when she mightn't ever show her face again.

Christina had no place in his life on Maple Island and he certainly wasn't going to let her spoil his quality time with Summer when they were so early into a possible relationship. The best way to put his ex-wife far from his thoughts was to focus on the woman with him now, who would never do anything to hurt him or Gracie.

By engaging her in another breath-stealing kiss, it wasn't long before he was led astray by the taste of her and knowing she was his for the entire night. With one hand tangled in her hair, the other possessively around her waist, he backed her towards his bedroom.

'Dr Valdez, I'm afraid I don't have any pyjamas to wear for our sleepover,' Summer murmured against his lips.

'That's okay. For what I have in mind you're not going to need any.'

Summer knew he was trying to take both their minds off the woman she'd seen him with today. It was working. When he was sucking her bottom lip into his mouth, undressing her painfully slowly and taking his time to kiss every inch of skin he uncovered, she didn't want to think about any other woman. Especially not the one he'd thought he'd spend the rest of his life with. He'd assured her he hadn't been interested in anything his ex had to say or offer, and she had to believe him because the alternative would break her heart. Tonight she wanted to enjoy time with *her* man and there was no room for another woman in their bed.

Summer slid her hand over his crotch and staked her claim on the hard evidence it presented that it was definitely her he wanted.

Rafael exhaled a hot breath in response. 'Summer, we've got all night.'

'You promised we weren't going to be needing clothes.' She undid his fly. 'So I'm simply making sure you stick to your word.'

Her bold move prompted a flurry of mutual undressing until all she was wearing was a coy smile.

The invitation to spend the night marked a progression in their dynamic. He didn't do anything without a lot of thought behind it and he was showing her he was thinking of her as part of his family.

The thought should have terrified her after the loved ones she'd lost in the past, but Rafael wouldn't have let her get so close if he wasn't serious about them having a future together. Their relationship had evolved so naturally she hadn't seen it coming. She mightn't have intended it to happen, or been ready for it, but she was becoming part of this family and she didn't want her insecurities spoiling it now.

They tumbled onto the bed, desperate to make that final connection. Looking into Rafael's eyes, she could see the moment he entered her was as gratifying and meaningful to him as it was to her.

It was too early to say she loved him, or to expect it in return, but she felt it every time their bodies joined together. As he made love to her, Summer was powerless against the waves of pleasure carrying her ever forward towards paradise. She clamped her hand over her mouth, knowing she couldn't hold back voicing her pleasure when the final wave hit.

Rafael peeled her hand away from her mouth but didn't slow his quest for her orgasm. 'I want to hear you.'

That demand was all it took to tip her over the edge, her body shuddering simultaneously with the cry of ecstasy ripped from her. Again and again Rafael hit that sweet spot and triggered a succession of repeated responses until she had nothing left to give before he finally indulged his own satisfaction with one last vocal thrust.

As they spooned together atop his bed, her body satiated and her mind at peace, she let herself drift towards slumber. She'd tried the single life, told herself she'd be happier on her own safe from the pain of risking another relationship, but it simply couldn't compare to lying here with Rafael's arms wrapped around her.

Today he and Gracie had shown her all she had to gain from having them in her life, everything she'd missed growing up and had thought could hurt her after Marc. The fun of a family day out ending with sharing a bed with her lover was no match for going home to an empty house.

If this was a dream she never wanted to wake up. Unless it was to a naked Rafael and the promise of a home-cooked breakfast.

Opening her eyes to see Rafael next to her with the early morning sun shining through the window was bliss compared to those mornings lying in bed staring at the ceiling until it was time to get ready for work. She'd be content to lie here all day.

'Morning.' He scooted close enough to her that she could feel his erection pressed against her.

'Morning.' She didn't open her eyes and simply snuggled back into him.

Rafael cupped her breast in his hand, rolling her nipple between his thumb and forefinger until her body stirred with arousal. She gave a happy purr and let him continue the wake-up call, his hand travelling down to find the warmth between her legs. He slipped a finger easily inside her and Summer sighed as he began stroking her, stoking the embers of last night's fire back into life.

As he increased the rhythm of his ministrations she was writhing against him in ecstasy, desperate to find that welcome release. With great effort she finally opened her eyes and turned around so she could see his face and kiss his lips. His erection grazed against her as she shifted position and it was apparent he was in need of some relief too.

She straddled those muscular thighs she'd fantasised about so often and sank slowly down onto his thick shaft, revelling as he filled her so completely. With her hands on his chest she ground her hips into him, savouring the feel of him inside her. Hands on her buttocks, lips at her breast, Rafael thrust into her, filling her to the brim until she was ready to burst. As sensation overtook her, limbs trembling with her impending climax, Rafael took charge, rolling her onto her back and pumping into her relentlessly. Their lazy morning in bed quickly became a frantic pursuit of mutual gratification. Her cry was drowned out by Rafael's primal growl as he gave himself completely to her.

With heaving chest and panting breath, Summer smiled at him. 'I wouldn't mind that kind of wake-up call every day.'

'It certainly beats my usual exercise routine.' Rafael laughed through his laboured breathing, equally exhausted by their early morning workout.

'I hope that doesn't mean Triathlon Dad is

hanging up his running shoes and swimming trunks. I wouldn't want to disappoint your legion of female admirers waiting to see you in all your glory. For some of us the sight of you in very little is the highlight of our day.' Now she had intimate knowledge of what lay beneath his clothes she had a lot more to be thankful for.

She danced her fingertips around his nipple, delighted he'd found another outlet for all that energy.

'I can think of much better ways to get sweaty.' His throaty growl travelled all the way down Summer's body, immediately reawakening that need for him.

'You're insatiable.' She giggled as he slid his body over to cover hers, apparently already sufficiently recovered from the last event.

'Only for you.' He covered her face and neck in swoony butterfly kisses to drive her wild.

The baby monitor on his nightstand suddenly crackled into life with the sound of a certain three-year-old getting restless to start her day.

Rafael groaned. 'Perfect timing as usual, Gracie.'

'We can't complain. She's been very good. As has her father.' Summer gave him a playful slap on the bottom, aware their sexy time was over. Gracie expected to see her at breakfast but not in her father's bed.

As she moved to get dressed, Rafael lay back to watch. 'We don't have to commit to anything formal but I would like you to stay over here whenever you can.'

He was being deadly serious and though the suggestion made Summer's heart pick up an extra beat at the thought of sharing his bed on a regular basis, she remained wary. The last time she'd jumped in with both feet she'd had to change jobs and move to an island to get over it.

'Let me think it over and I'll have my people get back to you.' She kept the tone light so he wouldn't take offence that she wasn't leaping at the chance.

'You do that.' Thankfully he appeared confident enough in his prowess to know she wouldn't be able to resist.

'In the meantime, I think your daughter and your house guest are expecting some breakfast.' It was going to be a rush to get home, showered and changed in time for work but she wasn't going to miss sitting down to a cosy family breakfast together. Something she hadn't experienced in a very long time.

'You're in a good mood.' Alex interrupted Rafael's whistling to comment on the huge grin he hadn't been able to wipe off his face today.

'It does happen occasionally.' Rafael closed the patient files he was reading at the nurses' station, unwilling to get drawn into a conversation about the reasons behind his current exuberance. Usually after battling to get Gracie ready and fit in a swim he had a fraught start to the working day. It was a completely different experience having Summer there in the morning.

Her presence hadn't made his daughter any more co-operative but with Summer's help and calming influence he hadn't found it as stressful as he normally did. The memory of their incredible night, and morning, in his bed had probably helped his mood too. He didn't want to scare her off, and it was early days, but he'd meant what he'd said about having her there on a regular, hopefully even permanent, basis.

He'd spent the last couple of years being careful, guarding his heart along with his daughter's, and it had very nearly cost him the best thing to happen to him since Graciela. Yes, he'd been burned before but so had Summer and she wouldn't have embarked on this affair to play games with his affections when she knew how that felt. He'd give her whatever time and space necessary to be sure he and Gracie were truly what she wanted because he already knew she was the one for him.

He was living, enjoying life, rather than simply surviving, which he'd been doing ever since he'd left Spain to come to America. Medical school had been his dream but it hadn't been easy, cut off from everything he'd ever known. He'd had to work hard to achieve his success with no emotional or financial support along the way.

He'd loved Christina but their time together had been marred by arguments and their clashing views on what married life should entail. For him it had been about settling down and having a family but she hadn't believed it should curtail her love of partying. When Gracie had come along Rafael had been overwhelmed by love for their child, but bringing a baby into their marriage had only added to their problems when Gracie had demanded more attention than her mother had been prepared to give her.

Looking back now, he could see she'd only agreed to start a family for his sake. He was thankful for the joy it had brought him but it had come at the price of their marriage. Christina hadn't been ready for motherhood, if she'd ever really wanted it. This time spent with Summer had shown him what family life could be like with someone supporting them both. Someone they both loved in return.

This wasn't post-sex daydreaming. Summer was everything he could ever want in a partner—she was smart, kind, caring and had proved she'd be there for them come what may. It was natural she should be cautious about rushing into this but he was prepared to wait, content with his life on the island. In the meantime, he'd woo her the old-fashioned way, with hearts and flowers and whatever it took for her to believe the strength of his feelings for her.

He pulled out his cellphone to text her on his way to his next clinic.

Thinking about you. xx

A reply pinged back before he could switch his phone off.

In that case you should take a cold shower ;)

He laughed out loud then had to check and make sure he hadn't disturbed anyone nearby. Thankfully everyone else was too busy to notice him sexting Summer.

Why don't you take one with me later? Dinner at mine tonight. Don't forget your toothbrush. xx

What? No PJs? :)

Rafael smiled at the screen, the image of Summer, naked in his bed, burned into his brain for ever and putting him in danger of spending the rest of the day in physical discomfort until he was able to do something about it.

Perhaps for the bedtime-story-reading part of the evening but not for the adults-only section. I want you naked.

He groaned. He was going to have to end this flirting by text before he got into trouble wishing the day away.

Ooh, very demanding, Señor Valdez. Now break's over. We'll have to save the rest of our fun for tonight. xx

He turned his cell off and put it in his pocket or there'd be no chance of focusing on work this afternoon.

He was still smiling as he walked into his office. Although the good mood wore off pretty quickly when he saw who was waiting for him there.

'Christina? What on earth are you doing here?'

'*Hola*, Rafael. I thought it would be better if we spoke face to face instead of over the phone. Your work address was on the business card you gave me.'

She knew him too well. He'd had absolutely no intention of answering her calls or continuing a discussion with her. He didn't believe they had anything to say to each to her after all this time. They were strangers now. The Christina he'd known would never have followed him here but run in the opposite direction from the life he represented.

'I don't think there's anything you could possibly say that I want to hear.' That time had passed. Whatever explanation or feeble apology he'd expected two years ago literally didn't matter to him now. The deed had been done and he and Gracie had managed fine without her.

'Don't you think we have things to discuss?' She was sitting in his chair, her perfectly manicured hands resting on his desk as though she had every right to be there.

'Such as?' He wasn't going to play games and the sooner she got to the point the sooner he could get her out of here. She wasn't going to steal away his chance at happiness for a second time.

'Our daughter.'

All that warmth that had been spreading through his veins from his exchange with Summer now turned to ice. There was no way she was going to drop in now and upset things when she'd shown no previous interest. He wouldn't let her.

'I thought you'd forgotten you had one.' The bitterness he could still taste in his mouth suggested he hadn't quite got over her abandoning them.

Christina flinched at that one and displayed a hint of a conscience. 'I know I treated you both appallingly but I've done a lot of growing up since then. I did try to find you. I've missed you. Both of you.'

If she'd thought she could walk in here and he'd drop to his knees begging her to come back, she was deluded. Seeing her here today at least confirmed one thing, that he didn't love her any more. There had been that lingering doubt in the far recesses of his mind that he might harbour feelings for her—after all, he hadn't been the one to end their marriage— but there wasn't one part of him that was even slightly pleased to see her again.

'Up until a couple of months ago we were still living in the same house in Boston so you couldn't have missed us that much.' Life could've turned out so differently if she'd come back before he'd met Summer and discovered what true love felt like, but he was happy here. He'd moved on.

'You've every right to be mad at me, Raf. I wasn't a good wife to you, or a good mother to Graciela. I've only figured that out now when I see all of my friends getting married and set- tling down.'

Rafael sank down into the seat usually re- served for his patients during consultations, experiencing the same sort of dejection they probably did when he had to give them life- changing news. Whatever his personal views about her, Christina was still Gracie's mother. It was just a shame it had taken her so long to realise it.

'What exactly is it you want, Christina?' He

would fight tooth and nail to keep his daughter with him when he was all she'd ever known. There was no danger of him letting Christina take her away from him only to dump her when she got bored playing house again.

'To be a good mom to Gracie.' She ignored his snort of derision. 'She doesn't know me and I want to rectify that. I'm hoping she's young enough not to remember the past so we can start over again.'

'I'll need more than that to convince me this isn't simply a whim and you'll walk away from Gracie when you get bored again.' This was exactly what he'd known she would do when he'd seen her again—rock up and ruin everything he had going here.

'Okay, cards on the table.' He could see her swallow hard, looking uncomfortable about whatever she was about to divulge, but he took no satisfaction in it when it could be potentially life-changing for all of them. 'Recently, I've found out my chances of conceiving again are small. Graciela was something of a miracle, although I didn't know it at the time. Seeing you again, well, it made me think of everything I'd lost.'

'You didn't lose us, you tossed us aside like trash.' He didn't want to get taken in by her crocodile tears if this was nothing more than an exercise in self-pity.

'I'm sorry. You'll never know how sorry I am for my behaviour. All I can say is that I wasn't mature enough to handle the responsibility of having a family.'

'And now you are?'

'I like to think so.' She gave him a watery smile. 'I realise how precious it is these days. Since seeing you, I haven't stopped thinking about Gracie and wondering what she's like. She'll be a proper little person now.'

Thinking of what a real character his daughter was did make him smile. 'Yes, she is.'

'Who does she look like?'

'Me.' It had made it easier for him that she'd clearly inherited his family features rather than being a clone of her mother and reminding him every day of the woman who'd broken his heart.

'I don't suppose you have a photograph?'

Suddenly this was becoming all too real, with Christina showing an interest in the child he'd raised on his own all this time.

'Look, this is a lot to dump on me. We have a good life here without you.' It was all he could do not to tell her he was with someone else now. Not to save Christina's feelings but to stop Summer getting caught up in this whole mess of his failed marriage when she was the symbol of the bright future available to his family.

'She's my daughter too, Raf. I don't want to get into a custody battle with you, but I do have rights as her mother. I'd prefer it if we could come to some sort of arrangement between us.

She might have a right to see her daughter but discussing custody of the child he'd raised alone for so long was something so momentous it deserved more time than he had in between appointments at work. Not only would he need time to think through the implications of letting her back into their lives in any capacity, he'd have to get some legal advice too. Introducing any change into Gracie's world would be a huge undertaking and even letting Christina have access was only something he would do when he was one hundred percent sure his ex-wife's intentions were long term.

He got up and opened the door to indicate he wanted her to leave. 'Not here and not now. I have work to do and patients to see.'

Christina sighed. 'Can we make an appointment to continue this discussion later? I'm not leaving the island until we do.'

He'd forgotten how stubborn she could be when she didn't get her own way, and an ex-wife stalking his every move wasn't going to make him an attractive prospect for Summer.

The breath he huffed out as he returned to the desk to scribble down his address was born of frustration and resignation that he was going to have to see her again no matter how unappealing that was to him. 'I'm not promising anything but if this is the only way I can get you to leave—'

'It is.' Christina took the scrap of paper with a triumphant grin but at least it prompted her towards the exit.

If she intended staying on Maple Island for any length of time it was going to be awkward for Summer. Christina wouldn't take too kindly to someone else taking her place in the family, regardless of her absence, her fiery temper a contrast to Summer's stable influence, which he'd come to cherish. Too bad. If it came to choosing sides he'd always take the path best for his family and that would lead him directly to Summer. Christina didn't stand a chance.

CHAPTER NINE

SUMMER COULDN'T WAIT. If she didn't manage to sneak in a quick Rafael fix to satisfy the craving she'd worked up with those text messages, there was no way she'd be able to concentrate on anything.

She'd managed to grab five minutes out of the nursery on the pretext she had to consult him on the matter of Gracie's pick-up today. It wasn't a complete fabrication since he hadn't given her a definitive time frame for their romantic evening and it might be easier for her to bring Gracie home straight after work.

She knew she couldn't keep on this way, texting and snatching moments with him during working hours. Sooner or later people would notice and start to talk and they couldn't keep their relationship quiet for ever on this small island. They couldn't exactly gag Gracie either if she chose to tell anyone about their *sleepover*.

Besides, she was fit to explode with happiness at the turn their relationship had taken and that wouldn't go unnoticed for long with her co-workers, who didn't think she had a life beyond her job. She was beginning to believe that all this time she'd spent alone was so she'd appreciate having Rafael and Gracie all the more. It was amazing how much joy there was to be had in simple things like a day out or having a meal in company.

Despite voicing her concern about spending too much time at their house, she knew she was too far gone to help herself. She wanted to spend every waking moment with Rafael, as well as the sleeping ones. He was so protective of his daughter he wouldn't have issued the invitation if he didn't whole-heartedly believe she would be a permanent feature in their lives.

That thought was both exhilarating and terrifying. Whilst she considered herself lucky to have found someone so loving and willing to share the most precious thing in his life with her, opening her heart left her more exposed to harm, compared to the protected life she'd led these past months on her own.

Hopefully, they'd have an opportunity to discuss what it was they both expected out of this relationship later and put her mind at ease that getting into something serious with him wasn't simply a step closer to heartache. For now, she'd be content to catch a minute or two alone with him. A quick kiss would be enough to carry her through the rest of the day on cloud nine.

Her pace increased with anticipation the closer she came to his territory, her heart beating that much quicker and the smile on her face becoming broader. It was amazing the effect a new relationship could have on a person, though she was sure he'd always possess the ability to send her body into raptures without having to lay a finger on her.

As she turned the corner into his department she paused to check her reflection in one of the glass panels lining the corridor. He'd seen her at her worst with bed head and yesterday's mascara smeared under her eyes. Her hair tied up in a ponytail and minimal make-up was essential for work and would have to do for now, but if she had some time later she'd prefer to go to a little more effort for their first *official* date.

When she found him waiting in the doorway of his office she was tempted to push him back through the door and ravish him on the desk she was so overcome with lust at the sight of him.

'I couldn't stop thinking about you.' She had her arms open, about to throw them around her man, when she saw a tall figure over his shoulder and composed herself again. The second she recognised Christina she could feel every painful splinter as her heart shattered.

'Who is this?' Although Christina addressed Rafael, she was clearly referring to Summer. As she looked her up and down, assessing her with a critical eye, Summer couldn't help but feel inadequate compared to this well-dressed, flawlessly made-up beauty. Rafael had dismissed their encounter altogether but she'd followed him here, proving she had some serious unfinished business with him.

'This is Summer Ryan. She's our child life specialist and nursery assistant at the clinic.'

Not 'my girlfriend', 'partner', or even 'friend'. A matter that wouldn't have bothered her if he was introducing her on a professional level, but they were supposed to be in a relationship now.

The unwelcome embodiment of her fears held out a hand for her to shake. 'Christina Valdez. Rafael's wife.'

The white noise was so loud in Summer's head she barely registered Rafael's correction. 'Ex-wife.'

'Sorry. I didn't realise you had company.' She turned away, tears beginning to blur the edges of Rafael's frame in the doorway. When he didn't reach out to try and stop her leaving, they fell in earnest.

'We'll talk later.' His words were a promise he'd see her again but not any more than that. She was clearly an outsider here, not included in their discussion of the future.

This should've been the start of their life together but with Christina back in the picture Summer's own position in his life was in jeopardy. She'd been here before, and knew she couldn't possibly compete with the mother of a man's child. It was a bond she could never hope to replicate or interfere with. Not that she ever would.

That threat she'd feared most was real now but she was in too deep to come out of this without adding a few more scars. She knew how this played out. Once the ex made it clear she was open to a reconciliation Summer would become a cuckoo in the nest. Christina was a real part of the family she could never call her own.

Even if they didn't get back together she was going to be gradually pushed out of her relationships with Rafael and Gracie when Christina claimed higher priority in the pecking order.

She didn't know why Christina had come back but she did know it was bad news for her. Summer was the poor substitute for a missing wife and mother, second best, and faced with a choice a single dad would choose to save his family.

She couldn't blame anyone for that decision when a child was involved. If she hadn't come to the island and her ex had wanted to try again she might have chosen familiarity over the unknown quantity of a new relationship. With Christina back on the scene she didn't know if she would have a future for herself with the Valdez family. It was a difficult decision to make but she wondered if it would be best to end things now, instead of waiting for Rafael to come to the same conclusion when she was in too deep to ever recover from the loss.

Although the idea she was saving herself from more pain than she was currently experiencing wouldn't soften the blow of letting him go now.

'What are you painting for us today?' She forced some brightness into her tone so Gracie wouldn't pick up on the fact something was wrong when she went back into the nursery unit. This was for her father to explain, not her, even if she had a clue what was going on.

'Boat,' the little girl said, as though it was as plain as day what the splodges on the paper represented.

Then it became clear that the three multicoloured splats on the paper were supposed to be the three of them yesterday on their trip. Summer swallowed back the wail she wanted to release at the injustice of the new loss she was to suffer.

Rafael was walking on shards of glass, pacing the room as he waited for Summer to arrive. She'd barely glanced in his direction when he'd gone to pick Gracie up from nursery. Not that he blamed her. There was so much they had to talk about but at the time he'd simply wanted to put some space between her and Christina.

That's why he hadn't been in any hurry to inform his ex about Summer's real identity as his new partner. He wouldn't put it past her to try and make trouble through pure jealousy. Her pride would decree it if Christina thought she'd been replaced. Which she most certainly had.

Tonight was supposed to have been romantic, something for Summer and him to look forward to when they could simply enjoy each other's company in private. Now he knew they were going to have to spend the evening discussing his ex-wife, what she was doing here, and how he was determined not to let her interfere in their personal business. That was before they came up with a plan of how to introduce her back into Gracie's life with minimal disruption.

All of this could only be achieved if Summer forgave him his earlier brusqueness to show up here for dinner. With Gracie already in bed they'd be able work through any problems in peace and quiet, and pick up from where they'd left off this morning. Preferably back in his bed, leaving the rest of the world outside the door.

His confidence in their relationship had been knocked by Christina's arrival, as he was sure Summer's had. An ex-wife was a reminder of all the ways in which he'd failed as a husband and a partner. Whatever her reasons for leaving, he hadn't been enough for her to stay and he couldn't be sure it would be any different with Summer.

In an effort to convince her that despite the evidence of one failed relationship he was worth a chance, he'd pulled out all the stops tonight with a home-made seafood paella and sangria for his seduction attempt. He wanted Summer to remember there was more to him than work and emotional baggage.

He lit the candles in the centre of the dining-room table and when the rap on the door finally came, he poured two glasses of fruit-infused red wine to help them both unwind. Until then he hadn't been sure she'd keep their date.

'I'm so glad you came—' His relief was short-lived when he found Christina standing on the doorstep instead of Summer.

'Hello, Rafael.'

'Christina, now is not the time,' he said, making no effort to hide his disappointment.

'You're the one who gave me this address.' She shrugged and pushed past him into the house. He followed her, without even bothering to close the door because as far as he was concerned she'd be going straight back through it once he caught up with her.

'We're going to have to discuss boundaries and the importance of sticking to a schedule if you want this to work,' he said with a frown.

She helped herself to a glass of sangria and

made herself comfortable on his couch. 'So, you do agree we need to sort out an arrangement for me spending time with Gracie?'

If she'd arrived a week ago he would've said under no circumstances but events had made him re-evaluate decisions like that and how they would affect Gracie. It shouldn't be down to him to deny them from getting to know each other. Perhaps it was about time Christina realised how wonderful their daughter was but not right now when Summer was supposed to be on her way over.

'I'll agree to think about introducing you but not tonight. She's in bed.'

'Can I at least pop in and see her?'

'No. If you wake her it'll take all night to settle her again. I promise I'll sort something out so you can meet her but I really need you to go.' She had no clue about Gracie's needs and it was going to take time to understand them, if she was willing to put in the effort. That wasn't something that could be taught, and so far Summer had been the only one who'd truly understood what it took to make a difference in Gracie's life, and his too.

'I'm so happy you've decided to give me another chance, Raf.' Christina bounced up from her seat to plant a kiss on his cheek and he could feel the glossy imprint of her lipstick stain his skin.

'Sorry, am I interrupting something?' A pale Summer stood at the door, watching their interaction, and Rafael immediately sprang away from his ex-wife, feeling guilty for even having her in the house.

'Christina just stopped by to talk about Gracie. She's going now.' Rafael stared daggers at Christina, willing her to take the hint that she'd outstayed the welcome he'd never issued in the first place.

'No, you stay, Christina. I'll go.' Summer turned on her heel and walked back out the door without any further discussion. This was not the seduction he'd had in mind.

'I had no idea she was coming here tonight,' he said, chasing after her.

'What is it she wants? What is it you want, Rafael?' This time she did meet his gaze but all he saw in her eyes was uncertainty, replacing the desire he'd seen there earlier today.

'She says she wants to be part of Gracie's life again and to make up for her mistakes. I have to think of what's best for my daughter.' He didn't want anyone to get hurt and believed the only way to handle this was if they all worked together.

'Two parents.' Summer agreed with the conclusion he'd come to too. He didn't want or need Christina in his life but it wouldn't be fair for Gracie to suffer because of their issues.

'How's that going to work when you're here and Christina's in Boston?'

'We haven't figured that out yet.'

'You're seriously thinking of moving back? For Christina?'

'I want to do whatever's best for Gracie.' He didn't want to uproot her but the arrangements were going to prove tricky. The first step was at least to agree she could meet her mother.

'I see…' Summer reached up and rubbed at the spot where Christina had kissed him earlier.

'Summer, it's not how it looks.' He scrubbed

at the lipstick evidence of his ex-wife's over-exuberance and cursed his bad luck. It was understandable Summer was upset when their supposed romantic evening had ended up with Christina firmly in the middle of it but he had no interest in any other woman. He thought she knew that.

'You're Gracie's parents. It's probably best if I let you two work things out between you.' With that, she walked out of the house and disappeared off into the night.

'Summer, come back. There's nothing going on between us. Summer…' he called out into the darkness, hoping his word was enough for her. It wasn't as though he could rush out and explain things, leaving Gracie here by herself. Summer knew that and by walking away she wasn't leaving any room for discussion.

He felt bereft standing in the doorway, waiting for her to come back once she'd cooled off, but she didn't. He wasn't sure if her parting words pertained to cancelling their dinner or their whole relationship. Christina was Gracie's mom and it was inevitable Summer would feel slighted by her arrival when she'd done so much for the little girl, but it shouldn't have affected their relationship.

He tried to find comfort in the fact that he hadn't actually done anything wrong. Summer meant so much to him he wasn't going to let things end like this. If she wouldn't talk to him tonight he was going to make sure she heard him out tomorrow. On an island this small she couldn't avoid him for ever and he would track her to the ends of the earth to give their relationship a fighting chance. He just hoped she felt strongly enough about him to put up with the hassle of having his ex in the picture.

He'd opened his home, his family and his heart to her, believing she was the one who could love him and Gracie without conditions, and prayed this wasn't a sign she'd turned tail and run at the first hurdle, rather than tackle it with him.

Perhaps a painful break-up had been inevitable. That wouldn't make it any easier to accept losing the woman he loved.

Summer stumbled down the steps blinded by the tears she worried would never stop. Rafael had sworn he'd never hurt her and he was doing the same thing Marc had done by putting his ex before her. Despite his insistence nothing was going on, she'd heard Christina thanking him for giving her a second chance and seen the evidence of her kiss on his cheek. He hadn't come after her or put up any sort of fight for her, much less considered her feelings about any of this. Perhaps he was hedging his bets by keeping both of them onside but she'd already been pushed out of the decision-making that would affect her life as much as everyone else's.

If she threw away everything she'd built for herself on Maple Island on a man who could cast her aside when the mood took him then she obviously hadn't learned her lesson well enough the first time around.

CHAPTER TEN

'DO YOU WANT me to clean that off your fingers, Gracie?' Summer tried to get her to communicate her needs verbally as she held up her hands, crying about the pieces of modelling dough sticking to her skin, but recently she seemed to be having trouble to adequately express her feelings.

She picked off the bigger pieces herself and took a cloth to wipe off the rest. Tears pricked her eyes as she tended to the little girl who was now only her ward on a professional basis. It had been a tough couple of weeks for them both but at least Summer had an idea of what was going on. She had no clue what Gracie had been told about why she'd stopped coming around or about Christina's arrival in her life, but the disruption had set back her progress. Something she knew neither she nor Rafael would have wanted for her.

'All clean for your father coming.' The words almost stuck in her throat as she saw Rafael and Christina walking towards the nursery unit, coming to get their daughter to complete the happy family picture.

She had known Christina was still on the island as the rumour mill was working overtime about the mysterious woman spending time with Dr Valdez. It didn't give her any satisfaction that she was the only one aware of her real identity when it was the reason for ending her relationship with Rafael.

She hadn't seen her face to face since that last night at Rafael's place when her whole world had come crashing down around her. If she'd had any doubts she'd done the right thing it had been confirmed by the fact he'd chosen to stay with Christina rather than come after her. She'd lain awake the whole night crying, tormented by the image she had of the two of them sharing the candlelit dinner meant for her.

Since then the only contact she'd had with Rafael had been here at the nursery during Gracie's handover, which had been limited to stilted conversation over his child's progress and nothing more. That was entirely her doing. Rafael had tried calling, texting and had attempted to explain his actions, but she'd blocked him at every turn. She didn't need to hear excuses when Christina was still here and very much part of their lives.

Although she would admit to missing him, spending time with him and Gracie and generally being part of the family. There should be some relief to be found that they had never got around to signing contracts regarding Gracie's full-time care when it would be excruciatingly painful watching them bond as a family from the outside and see them sail off into the sunset.

She'd felt so alone all of a sudden she'd even made attempts at rebuilding her relationship with her mother. They spoke on the phone most days now and she was thankful she had someone who would still be there for her no matter what. If things here finally got too much she might think about taking an extended vacation to spend some time with her mom and her stepdad, getting to know them again. It seemed to have worked for Christina.

By all accounts Christina was renting a property on the island so she wasn't in Rafael's house full time, probably to ease Gracie into the idea of her being there before they made anything permanent. Summer believed it was just a matter of time and the thought they might even consider moving back to Boston was enough to keep her awake at night. It was torture watching them all grow closer as she faded from memory.

'Hey, how's my girl?' He forced a hug on his daughter but she kept her eyes firmly on Christina, who was standing hesitantly beside him.

'We've had quite a day, playing with the modelling clay.' Summer pointed towards the table where she'd been rolling and cutting out multicoloured butterfly shapes before mashing them all together and starting again. That creation and destruction had held her attention for most of the day and she'd protested when Summer had attempted to introduce her to a new activity. In the end she'd capitulated and joined her at the table, the repetitive action surprisingly calming. She might take the mini rolling pin, clay and cutters home to keep her too occupied to wonder what the Valdez family were up to elsewhere.

'Your papa and I thought we could take you for a nice treat. I hear there's a lovely bakery down the street. Would you like to show me where it is?' Christina was crouched down and holding out her hand in the hope Gracie would want to go with her. To her credit, she didn't seem as though she was steamrollering her into a mother-daughter relationship. At Rafael's insistence she was slowly but surely building up that trust and easing her way into her daughter's life. The way Summer had been doing up until Christina's arrival on the island.

Gracie glanced at her for reassurance. 'Can Summer come too?'

The request twisted the dagger deeper into her heart when she wanted more than anything to remain part of this family, but her reasons for putting some distance between them hadn't changed. Even if her idea of self-preservation was painful now, it would save her in the long run.

'Yes, you're very welcome. Gracie talks about you a lot and we're very grateful for everything you've done for her.' Christina's thanks, though well meaning, did nothing to make Summer feel any more included. She didn't say that Rafael talked a lot about her and she was thanking her on their behalf, as a couple. Even Rafael looked awkward about the invitation.

What could she do but smile through her heartbreak when this was Gracie's mother and Summer knew what it was to go through life with that void left by absent family members. 'Thanks, but I'm needed here for a while longer. Enjoy your treat.'

When Gracie slowly reached out to take Christina's hand in hers and they walked off down the corridor, the moment was bittersweet for Summer.

'Thanks for doing that. Gracie's finding this a little difficult to come to terms with. As am I.' Rafael held back to speak to her and despite the appearance of having his family back on track he looked as miserable as she felt. If it wasn't all unicorns and rainbows at Casa Valdez, it made her sacrifice all the more tragic.

'It will take time. You know that. Wait and see. In another few months it will be as if you and Christina never split up and you'll be one big happy family.' Where that left her she didn't know because if this was any indication, she couldn't cope with seeing them all together on a daily basis. It was like rubbing salt in the open wound where her heart used to be. She was the ultimate loser in this game of happy families.

Rafael frowned at her. 'I don't want to get back together with Christina. I never did. I'm only tolerating her because she's Graciela's mother. It's not her I want, it's you. Nothing happened that night with her, or any other night, I swear. We've only ever talked about Gracie.'

'We've been through this, Rafael. I'm no longer part of the equation and the sooner you realise that the easier it will be for you to move on as a family.'

He wasn't making this any easier for her by telling her he wasn't over her when she'd been consoling herself with the idea that she was somehow saving his little family and giving Gracie the stability she herself had never had growing up.

When she'd walked in on that intimate moment between Rafael and Christina she'd seen the reunion between parents she'd always wanted as a child herself. Although it had almost killed her so soon after she and Rafael had got together, she had hoped something good would've come out of this whole sorry mess for Gracie.

Of course she wanted to believe him that he wasn't interested in Christina when there was still a candle burning for him in her very soul, but how long would that last when his family was growing closer by the day? She'd done the hard part in walking away and it would only reopen the wound if she let him close again.

'Gracie misses you too. I've tried to explain to her that you're giving her some space to get to know her mama but I can't expect her to understand when I don't know myself what the hell happened.' He made a move towards her but Summer immediately backed away. Not because she was afraid someone would see but because she didn't trust herself not to weaken if he touched her.

'That's not fair. You know I love Gracie but she's not my daughter, is she?' Outside this nursery Gracie was no longer her responsibility. That privilege was entirely her parents', and she wouldn't allow Rafael to use emotional blackmail to get around her defences. Not when she was on the verge of telling him she loved him too. That really would jeopardise Gracie's chance of growing up in a stable home with someone who wasn't paid to look after her interests.

Over his shoulder she could see the two figures coming back down the corridor, probably wondering what was keeping him.

'I think someone is waiting for you.' Summer pointed him in the direction he was most needed. Already she was making plans to run into the staffroom for the emotional breakdown that had been coming since she'd walked out of his house, her voice wavering with the sob she was trying to hold back. It was all too much today, seeing them together, the uncertainty in Gracie's face as she'd taken her mother's hand, and Rafael no less attentive towards her than he'd ever been.

If she'd done the right thing in letting him go to protect her heart then why did it feel so wrong?

Rafael waved at them then turned back towards her with one final comment before he left. 'I'm not giving up on us, Summer. Even if you have.'

She'd completely detached herself from him and Gracie since Christina had arrived at his house that night and she felt a huge sense of loss. They were professional and courteous to one another at the clinic but it was awful pretending that was all they'd ever been to one another. Any time he'd tried to apologise for what had happened or explain what had happened, he was met with the same response. That he shouldn't worry about her and to concentrate on his daughter. It was in his nature to do both when he wanted to find a way to have them both in his life.

Based on her relationship history he could

understand why she was so convinced he and Christina were trying to get their relationship back on track, but he liked to think after everything they'd shared Summer would give him a chance to prove his feelings for her.

He wasn't simply going to abandon what they'd had together over a misunderstanding, or because the damage their exes had done was getting in the way of them having a future together. They'd resisted their feelings for each other for far too long and things had only come to a head when they'd started working together outside the clinic. If she wasn't going to speak to him at work, there was one last reason she would have to see him and that was for the triathlon.

There was still a lot of red tape to sort out for the event and Summer had been the main driving force, courting publicity and participation since their parting of ways. She'd insisted she could manage on her own, regardless that it was supposed to have been about integrating him into the community as well as supporting the clinic.

Well, if it would force her to face the feelings she had for him and realise how much she meant to him, he was going to step up as co-creator of this enterprise. Whether she liked it or not, he loved her and he was going to make sure she knew it.

'Where did you put all the signed sponsor-ship forms and insurance papers?' Summer was trying not to let her temper get the better of her but she was stressed to breaking point, not only with the task of putting on this event, which seemed to have captured the interest of the entire island, but because Rafael was in-sisting on doing it with her.

They were in her house on the eve of the tri-athlon, making sure they had all eventualities covered because she thought it would be easier meeting at hers than at his, where Gracie and all the lovely memories she had there would be tarnished with Christina's presence. How-ever, she hadn't accounted for the claustropho-bia of having him under her roof and not being able to walk away from all the emotions that brought bubbling to the surface.

'They're right here.' He leaned over her

shoulder and sifted through the mass of print-outs and schedules to uncover the items she'd accused him of misplacing.

'Sorry, I must've set them down there earlier. I…er…have a lot on my mind.' Particularly how good he smelled, like soap and cologne, as if he'd just got out of the shower. She tried to stop her brain venturing there, giving her a vivid memory of what a naked Rafael looked like, and failed. There he was, muscles, abs and everything else on display as he soaped himself up…

'Too much on my mind,' she muttered. Once this triathlon was over that was it. She was putting a ban on him getting within hot-breath-on-her-neck distance.

'You need to relax.' He placed his hands on her shoulders and started to massage the bunch of knots her nerves had become. She hoped he didn't hear the little whimper that escaped as his strong hands kneaded her flesh for the first time since their break-up. It felt so good to have him touch her, firm, tender, and always with the goal of seeking her pleasure. She closed her eyes and let him work his magic until she knew she was in danger of getting carried away and forgetting they were supposed to be working. Rafael was no longer hers and her body was no longer his to manipulate. Even if she enjoyed it.

She shrugged him off. 'Okay, I'm relaxed now.'

'Everything's in place. You should really take some time out before you work yourself into the ground. We could open a bottle of wine and have a chat like old times if you'd like. Christina's keeping an eye on Gracie tonight.' He was still hovering beside her, putting her body on high alert as though it was waiting for another touch to send her back into raptures. Not even the mention of Christina could apparently dissuade her treacherous libido that this man wasn't any good for her, and she swore Rafael was doing this on purpose. It wasn't as if she didn't have any furniture for him to sit on.

'I don't think that's a good idea. You should be in training and I think we're done for the night anyway. If I think of anything else before tomorrow, I'm sure I can manage on my own.' She turned around with the intention of dismissing him and pointing him in the direction of the door but he was there, in her space again, so close her mouth was dry with anticipation over his next move. The flick of her tongue to wet her lips only succeeded in drawing his attention further and turned his eyes black with desire for her.

If she didn't still have that one little part of her refusing to let her forget every time someone had hurt her in the past she'd have melted right onto her dining-room table and let him take her there on top of all the hard work she'd undertaken to try and distract herself from thinking about him.

'Please, Rafael.' The teary plea was for him to stop because she knew she couldn't. It was enough for him to take a step back and let her breathe again.

'I know you still care for me, Summer, and I have never loved anyone the way I love you. Just remember that.'

He left then, leaving her gasping for air in between the sobs of frustration and pain. How could she ever forget when it was the first time he'd said the words and made her realise more than ever what it was she'd lost. Everything.

Rafael no more wanted to take part in this triathlon than he wanted to follow Christina back to Boston but it was his last shot to get close to Summer.

He watched her now at the far side of the pool, homing in on her in the midst of the whooping crowd as she corralled her day-care charges into the stands to watch the race. He waved to Gracie, who was holding her hand, but the only person waving back was Christina, sitting a few rows back. It was all he could do to nod an acknowledgement of her support when it wasn't hers he sought.

The starting pistol sounded and he launched himself into the water along with his other competitors. He knew he was up against it with the super-fit Alex and a determined Maggie Greene, a physio at the clinic and a gold-medal-winning ex-Paralympian athlete. Not to mention Rick Fleming, the English doctor in the rehab team and all the other members of staff keen to compete today. Although he didn't care about winning. It would be all he could do to simply get through this today. Swimming, or any of his other leisure pursuits, was no longer the alone time he'd once looked forward to. Now he had too much of it.

He'd tried to remind Summer what they'd had together but even that hadn't been enough to change her mind when she was clearly still hurting over what had happened. That fear gripped his heart again that he might not ever win her back and he had to remind himself to breathe before he drowned himself in front of everyone on account of his troubled personal life.

With a rolling turn at the end of the swimming lane he launched himself into another lap, wanting to get this over as soon as possible. He didn't realise he was first to finish until he hoisted himself out of the pool and turned to see the women in his life on their feet, cheering. Even Summer was giving him a sad sort of smile. One that said she was proud of him but was wary of letting him know.

It occurred to Rafael in that second how miserable they all were without each other. Summer was such a caring woman who wanted the best for Gracie as much as he did and would put the little girl's happiness before her own. She was determined they should be happy together as a family. What she had yet to realise was that she was their family. He needed to show her in some way, make a commitment to her so she could see she was as important to him as his daughter.

'Come on, Raf, give the rest of us a chance,' Rick called to him with a laugh as they jumped on the exercise bikes to complete the cycling. There weren't enough to go around all of the competitors so their times were being added to their other scores later. That didn't stop the crowd following to cheer them on, gathering around the competitors so there was no escape from the scrutiny. The 'Triathlon Dad' nickname didn't make him laugh any more when it summed up the man he'd been before Summer and the man he'd return to if she wouldn't take him back. When all he had outside work was Gracie and his leisure pursuits, and though he loved his daughter, he loved Summer too. He wanted to be known as her partner, lover and companion, along with the other roles he had.

If the only way she was prepared to talk to him or acknowledge his existence was through this sporting spectacle, he was going to give it his all. He wanted her to see he was doing it for her, that he wanted this to be a success, but most of all that she was his motivation to win.

His legs were pumping, racking up the miles on the clock, sweat beading on his brow with the effort, but his focus was only on one thing. Summer. She'd managed to position herself near the front of the throng with Gracie in her arms and he knew she was there for him. He locked eyes with her and neither of them looked away until the bell sounded to signal the finish. It was obvious there was no one else for either of them, they'd simply been too scarred by the past to face up to it. Once this race was over he was going to confront her once and for all and make her acknowledge those feelings she had for him.

Now all he had to do was complete the run-ning stage of the triathlon and reach the finish line, where he knew Summer and Gracie would be waiting for him.

Summer couldn't help herself. She just had to be close to him. They'd both put so much effort into getting this event organised, in bringing the community together, he deserved her support. After checking that the rest of the children were being supervised, that's how she justified shoving her way through the crowd at least.

He had accrued quite a fan club, who'd followed him from the pool to watch his progress in the other events, and she was sure it wasn't entirely down to his athletic ability. She was as aware as every hot-blooded woman in the room how handsome he was in or out of the water, in or out of her bed. Even now, drenched in sweat after his exertions, people were swarming around him in an effort to be close to him. She, on the other hand, had remained at a distance until now, telling herself she had no right to celebrate his achievements when they were nothing to do with her any more.

When he fixed her with that intense stare

and rendered everything going on around them invisible she knew it was pointless to continue denying her true feelings for him. She was sure even Christina had realised since she'd backed away, leaving her and Rafael staring lustfully at each other.

If his ex-wife hadn't remained in the picture it would all have been so much easier. She would've forgiven Rafael by now if she wasn't still afraid he'd leave her for his ex. As they all made their way to the running track she made sure she had another prime viewing spot, close enough to see Rafael but somewhere Gracie wouldn't get jostled by the other spectators. Although she was so busy waving the little Spanish flag Summer had helped her make in nursery, the noise and the crowd didn't seem to be bothering her.

The competitors lined up in the starting blocks and she could see Rafael searching the faces to find her. A smile brightened his face once he found her and a blush crept over her body at his renewed attention. He'd had a couple of weeks without her, plenty of opportunity for his feelings for Christina to resurface, but it was always *her* he was looking for, saving his smiles for. Rafael wasn't a player who'd do that simply because he knew she'd turn to mush every time he looked at her.

She had to face the fact that he loved her, not Christina, and she was damn sure she loved him right back. The hardest thing to come to terms with was having Christina as a permanent fixture in their lives if she did get back together with Rafael. There was no way around that when she was Gracie's mother. Summer had to accept that, and the only thing stopping her then would be her own hang-ups about being second best. Something Rafael had repeatedly told her wasn't true. She had to trust him if she was ever going to be happy again.

When the starting pistol went off, a roar went up around her as everyone cheered on their favourite amateur athletes.

'You can do it, Rick.' Fleur Miller, Dr Fleming's other half, was doing her cheerleader bit beside Summer, and she automatically wanted to prove her allegiance to the man she loved too.

'Come on, Rafael,' she shouted, hoping he

could pick her voice out among the rest when Rick seemed to be closing in on his lead. It wasn't clear if he'd heard her or not but he did begin to pull away and Summer's heart was in her mouth as the two sprinted to the end.

'Your daddy won, Gracie!' Summer celebrated with Gracie as her father crossed the finish line, arms held aloft in triumph.

'I want my papa.' The little girl twisted in her arms, demanding to be set down so she could run to him. Summer did so but took her hand to lead her there safely. An excited Gracie was the only thing he'd want to see at the end of that gruelling challenge.

'Well done.' She gave him a verbal pat on the back as they went to meet him.

'Thanks.' He was doubled over, trying to catch his breath, but at the sound of her voice he looked up and gave her a smile bright enough to light up that black hole where her heart used to reside.

Gracie threw herself at him and regardless of his obvious discomfort he gathered enough energy to celebrate his win with his daughter.

'I'm not sure it's official yet, is it? The others couldn't have been too far behind.' As he said that, Rick crossed the line but Rafael had won every event so comfortably there was no doubt who was in first place overall.

'Trust me, you've got this,' Summer assured him, but even when they gave out the official announcement he was insisting Maggie should have been crowned the first triathlon winner. Due to a teenage bout of meningitis, the popular physio had lost both of her legs and had come a close second despite her prosthetics. However, the fiercely independent redhead had insisted that she shouldn't be given any special treatment or advantage over the others.

She seemed quite happy with simply finishing, kissing and hugging Alex and pulling his little boy into their celebrations as though they'd won the Olympics. Summer envied their happiness in contrast to the awkwardness between her and Rafael as he was awarded his gold medal. She wanted to do all those things too but she'd forfeited that position in his life, even though he had no one else to fill it. Christina, who, it seemed, was learning the patience and understanding it took to secure a place in her daughter's life, was also hovering uncertainly in the background.

'I'm giving this to the person I love most in the whole world,' he said, as he unhooked the medal and hung it around Gracie's neck. Summer wanted to be so much more than a spectator in their special moment. Her throat was raw with the effort of holding back the emotions she wanted to unleash.

'Congrats again. Sorry, I'll have to go and set up the course for our own mini-triathlon this afternoon.' She left Gracie with her father and the rest of the nursery staff, worried that she'd left it too late to patch things up with him.

'Good girl, Gracie!' Summer was supposed to be impartial for these things and this was supposed to be more about participation than competition, but she'd gravitated towards Rafael and Christina on the sidelines rather than taking an official role. It was impossible not to cheer Gracie along beside the other proud parents because that's exactly how Summer felt, watching her blossom. She'd grown from that anxious child who couldn't bear to be parted from her father to this absolute force of nature who was following the example she'd seen this morning and going hell for leather across the course. Even if paddling in a pool to collect a rubber duck and riding a tricycle across the grassy play area outside the nursery wasn't quite on the same level as the clinic triathlon.

'I can't believe how well she's doing. Her focus and co-ordination alone are amazing.' Rafael came to stand next to her, clapping and cheering his daughter on as she moved confidently from one stage to the next as directed by the staff.

'She has a great role model.' Summer had no doubt this display was in direct correlation to the one Gracie had watched her father triumph in and was eager to replicate it. Rafael had double the reason to be proud of his achievements today.

'I'd say she has two. You've done so much for her since we came to Maple Island. Summer, I—' He turned his attention away from his little athlete to look at her, the sudden wrinkle in his brow indicating he wanted to speak about something serious, and Summer swallowed hard at the thought she was going to have to stop avoiding the subject of their relationship.

Rafael took Summer's hand and made it obvious to anyone who was watching that he wanted to be with her. She had to stop pretending she believed otherwise and abandon her fears if she was ever going to find happiness.

She took a deep breath. 'It's been a joint enterprise in getting Gracie to reach this milestone and I want to be at your side, watching her grow and flourish. Today has reminded me that wherever you are is exactly where I need to be too. You've both taught me to grab life by the horns and go for what I want most in life, and that's you, Rafael.'

'You mean that? You have no idea what it did to me when I thought I'd lost you for ever. Please don't ever do that to me again.' He cradled her hand against his cheek and she knew she'd hurt him by trying to protect herself, thinking she knew what he wanted better than he did. Today he'd shown her beyond all doubt what it was he wanted and it was about time she stopped comparing him to Marc.

She was more than a convenience or a glorified babysitter to Rafael—if anything, she'd definitely been an inconvenience when she'd butted into his life. Even when they'd been on a break he hadn't given up on her. Thank goodness he could be as stubborn as she could when it was called for. 'I promise.'

'I want that in writing.'

Summer couldn't blame him for being wary when she'd denied those feelings for so long but she never wanted to be apart from him again.

The cheers went up as all the children completed the challenge but there was special recognition from Gracie's supporters that she'd been so adept at everything set before her. Since the participants were too young for the concept of competition they were all awarded medals, but Gracie stared at hers forlornly.

'What's wrong, Gracie? You did so well. We'll have to display your medal next to mine on the mantelpiece.' Rafael did his best to lift her spirits but she was still staring at her prize, lost in thought. Summer supposed that she was smart enough to realise it was a plastic replica and not the real deal like her father's.

'I think someone might have to stop at Brady's Bakery for a celebratory treat today.' She tried to raise a smile too without success, then Gracie said what was really on her mind.

'Can I have another medal?'

'Sure.' Summer retrieved the bag of leftover prizes and handed over an extra reward since she deserved it. 'Is this for Dolly?'

Gracie frowned at her. 'No. Papa said you give medals to people you love most.'

With that she gave Rafael the one hung around her neck and gifted the other right back to Summer. The sob was out of Summer's mouth before she could stop it, the gesture so unexpected and lovely that all three adults had tears in their eyes. She crouched down so Gracie could hang it around her neck and Summer couldn't have been happier with real gold. This was priceless, bestowed with such love she really felt like part of the family.

As she glanced across at Christina she realised her joy had come at the other woman's expense. She was gulping and dabbing her eyes, fighting the opposite emotions Summer was experiencing with the gesture.

The rest of the parents and children had filtered back inside the nursery for the refreshments that had been laid on, leaving them to work out their complicated family issues with some degree of privacy.

'Christina, no one wants to hurt you.'

'Gracie just needs time to get to know you better.' Summer followed up Rafael's attempt to console his ex-wife but they'd used the phrase so often it sounded lame even to her. There was nothing that could be said to take away the pain of what Gracie's mother would take as a rejection when it was how Summer had felt when she'd thought Rafael was leaving her. Only the strength of Christina's feelings for her daughter would determine what she would do next.

It was a surprise, and unnerving, to see Christina smiling at her. 'You're lucky, you know. I was married to this guy and we both know how great he is and my daughter loves and trusts you. I was a fool to let them go but it's you they love. I know they're both miserable without you, Summer. I guess I'll have to work on my relationship with Gracie some more. She's thriving here and, believe it or not, I want what's best for her.'

She shrugged her shoulders and led Gracie inside with the others for refreshments but Summer could sympathise with everything she'd lost when she'd come so close to losing it herself.

'Are you okay?' Rafael checked with her, though it was Christina whose heart was probably breaking.

'I'm fine. I just feel bad for her. After all she's Gracie's mom, she's always going to be part of your lives. She was right, though, that you're the best thing to ever happen to me. Did you mean it when you said you loved me?'

'Yes. I am totally, absolutely, crazily in love with you.'

'Good, because I love you too. Now make my dreams come true and tell me that in Spanish.'

'*Te amo.* Which is why I want you to marry me, Summer.'

'Pardon me?' She blinked at him, wondering if he'd taken a knock to the head during the triathlon.

'I know we haven't been together long but I'm happy to have a long engagement if that's what you need. You're the only woman I want to spend the rest of my life with and if you feel the same way I don't see why we should fight it. I want you, me and Gracie to be a family. For ever.'

The proposal of marriage was unexpected and wonderful and risky to even consider after all their troubles. But it was also the best reason she could think of to show how much faith she had in the relationship and the strength of her love for him. From now on she was focusing on the future, and the past was no longer going to dictate the decisions she made.

'Yes, I'll marry you, and Gracie. You're all I've ever wanted.' Summer had never imagined that coming to Maple Island would've been the answer to her prayers, but finally she felt complete. Now she was part of the loving family she'd always dreamed about.

EPILOGUE

'Do I NEED to curtsey or anything?' The prospect of meeting her in-laws for the first time was nerve-racking, not least because she'd come to learn how much of a big deal the Valdez family was in Spain. Rafael had almost been embarrassed by the column inches they'd taken up over the years in the Spanish glossy magazines when she'd done some research over the internet.

He was noticeably absent from the photographs of glitzy parties they'd thrown and attended over the years, but it was understandable when the man she knew was a world away from that kind of flashy lifestyle. She was nervous about meeting them when she was just a normal working woman and wondered if they'd consider her up to scratch for their son, and their family.

Rafael rolled his eyes at her as he loaded the cases into the car. 'I've told you, this is going to be all very low-key. They've been warned we don't want any fuss, especially for Gracie's sake.'

He was trying to downplay the significance of this but she knew it was an important step for him, introducing them to Gracie. Even though they'd been video-calling over the internet these past few months at her insistence, she could tell he was still worried that they might not accept their granddaughter.

'I suppose we have Christina to thank for this belated honeymoon.' She threw her arms around her husband's neck and kissed him, safe in the knowledge she'd never tire of kissing this gorgeous man for the rest of her days.

'We'll send her a postcard,' he said, and hugged her close.

Although they'd imagined a long engagement, things had kind of fallen into place when they'd realised what was important in their lives and both had come to the conclusion it was each other and a particular little girl.

They'd travelled back to Boston to get married in a private ceremony and surprised everyone with the news on their return. Life with Rafael and Gracie was chaotic and wonderful and she loved every moment of it. Since Christina had decided to stay on the island too, they had shared custody and it gave Summer and Rafael plenty of quality time together alone, making everyone happy.

The clinic had hired travelling nurse Stacey Ryder, who was softening Cody's hard shell with her arrival, so there was enough staff to cover their leave for a while. The only thing missing had been Rafael's family in Spain and, with Christina having already opened a dialogue, Summer had persuaded him to get in touch with them again.

He'd been surprised how emotional they'd been to hear from him and she thought perhaps a little sad at the time he'd lost with them. She understood that because of the half of her family she knew she'd probably never see again. However, she'd been making inroads into reconnecting with her mother, who doted on Rafael and Gracie almost as much as she did. She'd never expected to end up with such an extensive family but it was doing them all good to get to know one another again.

'We mightn't get time. After all, this trip is technically our honeymoon and Gracie's grandparents are very keen to babysit...' She trailed a finger down his chest and flicked open one of the buttons with her nail.

Rafael groaned and stilled her hand with his before she could tease him any more. 'It's a long flight, you know, and saying and doing things like that are going to make it very un-comfortable.'

'Sorry. I'm just looking forward to some alone time with you.' Although they'd packed everything they could think of to keep Gracie entertained on the journey, they both knew it was going to be challenging so she was already thinking ahead to the good part.

'I thought you might want to do some sight-seeing and touristy stuff?'

'We could do that or we could get some baby-making practice in,' she said, biting her lip. They hadn't discussed the idea of having children of their own but she thought having a sibling for Gracie would make their little family complete.

Thankfully Rafael looked delighted at the idea. 'Really? You want us to have a baby?'

Summer nodded.

'In that case, what are we waiting for? Let's hit the road!' He hurried her into the car, a great big smile plastered over his face, and the love she had for him almost bubbled over. She already knew what a great husband and father he was and another baby would be the icing on the cake for her perfect little family.

Coming to Maple Island had been the best move she'd ever made.

* * * * *

LET'S TALK

Romance

For exclusive extracts, competitions and special offers, find us online:

 facebook.com/millsandboon

@millsandboonuk

@millsandboon

Or get in touch on 0844 844 1351*

For all the latest titles coming soon, visit millsandboon.co.uk/nextmonth